McGEE AND ME!
THREE-BOOK COLLECTION

McGEE and me!

THE BIG LIE

A STAR IN THE BREAKING
THE NOT-SO-GREAT ESCAPE

MYERS / JOHNSON

Tyndale House Publishers, Inc.
Carol Stream, Illinois

Visit www.cool2read.com.

TYNDALE, Tyndale's quill logo, *McGee and Me!*, and the McGee and Me! character are registered trademarks of Tyndale House Publishers, Inc. The Tyndale Kids logo is a trademark of Tyndale House Publishers, Inc.

McGee and Me! Three-Book Collection

The Big Lie, A Star in the Breaking, and *The Not-So-Great Escape* copyright © 1989 by International Bible Society. All rights reserved.

Cover illustration copyright © 1989 by Morgan Weistling. All rights reserved.

Designed by Nicole Grimes

Scripture quotations are taken from *The Living Bible,* copyright © 1971 by Tyndale House Foundation. Used by permission of Tyndale House Publishers, Inc., Carol Stream, Illinois 60188. All rights reserved.

McGee and Me! Three-Book Collection is a work of fiction. Where real people, events, establishments, organizations, or locales appear, they are used fictitiously. All other elements of the stories are drawn from the author's imagination.

For manufacturing information regarding this product, please call 1-800-323-9400.

ISBN 978-1-4964-0329-2

Printed in the United States of America

21   20   19   18   17   16   15
7   6   5   4   3   2   1

M°GEE and me!

THE BIG LIE

BY BILL MYERS AND KEN C. JOHNSON

ONE

BEGINNINGS . . .

I pulled my space shooter from its holster. Time was running out. I had to reach my aircraft. The planet beneath me was about to go to pieces.

Just ahead of me lay a dark hallway filled with smoke. Live electric cables flipped wildly across my path. One touch from them meant total destruction—and that would mean no pizza for a long, long time.

Taking a deep breath, I leaped into the hall. The first cable hissed and crackled just over my head. I hurdled another cable, then another, and another. Finally the exit hatch lay just in front of me.

I stretched my hand toward the release handle. But a green slimy tentacle suddenly wrapped itself around my wrist. One of the guards must have hidden himself in the darkness.

"Prepare yourself for the worst," he gurgled.

"Hah!" I laughed, turning to face him. "I've already had lima beans in cream gravy. . . . Your threats don't scare me!"

But even as I spoke, another oozing tentacle curled around my throat. He pulled me off my feet and lurched forward. His face was hideous. And his wicked smile showed grimy teeth that had never seen a dentist.

I knew in a few more seconds I'd be dead. So I brought my space shooter up with lightning speed. "I've got no time to dance, frog-face," I sputtered through his choke hold. A blast exploded from my laser and consumed the green goon.

A rumbling sound below reminded me that my time was almost up. I had to get off this planet. I quickly bounded through the exit hatch. I reached the planet's surface and made for my aircraft.

As I leaped into the cockpit, the ground opened up in front of me. Fire shot up from the inside of this lost and dying world.

I hit the ignition. A bolt of fear shot through me as my engine coughed and sputtered. I didn't have any jumper cables, so I did what any good mechanic would do—I kicked the control panel. The engine roared to life!

I engaged the lifters and blasted into the star-filled sky.

As I reached orbit, the planet below exploded. A million meteors shot into the sky. I settled back for the trip home, satisfied. The formula for low-fat, freeze-dried pickles was tucked securely in my space jacket. *The world would again be a safer, if not thinner, place to live.*

Pretty exciting stuff, huh? But, believe it or not, that adventure was nothing compared to the one Nick and I were about to take. But I guess I'm getting a little ahead of myself.

My name is McGee. I came about through the talents and imagination of my best buddy, Nicholas Martin. You see, at the ripe old age of eleven, Nick is what you'd call a cartoonist. And we've been together from the first day he drew my adorable image on his sketch pad. And we stay together for good reasons. Sure, it's Nick who imagines and draws my amazing escapes (like the one I just mentioned). But it's me who makes sure my shy little pal finds the adventures in real life.

Adventures like those first few days at the new school—back when we all moved into Grandma Martin's house. And by "all," I'm talking about the WHOLE family. . . . First, there's Nick's older sister, Sarah. She's an okay kid, I guess—except she likes to give orders and mess with her hair a lot. Then, there's his kid sister, Jamie—a real cutie, full of energy, with a permanent ring of jelly around her mouth.

Then there's Nick's father, or "Mr. Dad" as I call him. He's a cool guy . . . honest, funny. And does he know his Bible? Let me tell you, Billy Graham's got nothing over this guy. He works as managing editor at the local newspaper, which gives me and Nick plenty of chances to get information to help solve crimes and stuff.

Then there's Mom. Like Grandma, she's smart as a whip and

spends lots of time helping people who have needs. She also makes great pancakes.

Last and most certainly least, there is a creature so awful words cannot describe him. In fact, his name says it all—"Whatever," the family dog. I think he's a cross between a Pekingese and a poodle. I'm not sure, but it comes out ugly any way you look at it. Besides, he sheds.

Anyway, about that adventure. It's probably best if I let you read it on your own. But don't worry. I'll be dropping in from time to time to make sure you get the facts straight—especially about the role I played in this, one of our greatest adventures.

It was six months ago that Mom and Dad had asked the family to think about moving in with Grandma. Everyone

was pretty excited. The kids had always loved the old house with its mysterious past. They loved the cellar. They loved the attic. And best of all they loved checking the loose bricks for hidden treasure and tapping the walls for secret passageways. So far, no luck. But that wouldn't stop them from trying.

Mom and Dad had other reasons for the move. . . .

First of all there was Grandma. As much as she hated to admit it, she was definitely getting older, and those stairs were definitely getting steeper.

Then there was the fact that Dad wanted to get the children out of the suburbs. It seemed that all that money and all that snobbery were starting to have an effect on the kids. "Half the world is starving to death," he said. "And the only thing our neighbors care about is who gives the best tennis lessons." Dad wanted the kids to be with real people who had real needs. "Let's put our faith into action," he said. "Let's see how we can help."

And finally there was Mom. Instead of her hectic teaching job, she felt that she should be spending more time with her family. "The kids won't be kids forever," she said. "I just want to be around in case they need me."

So . . .

Mom quit her job at the junior college.

Dad left his job as assistant editor at the *Tribune* and took over the small community paper.

And Grandma now had the entire family living with her.

Everything was perfect. Except for one small detail—no

one bothered to tell the kids how different life would be in the city.

Nicholas began to suspect it when his bike was stolen. It had barely made it off the moving van before it was gone.

And Sarah began to suspect it when she discovered that the nearest mall was almost ten miles away.

But that was only the beginning. . . .

Monday was hectic. Grandma's kitchen hadn't seen such activity in years. The Martin children and Mom and Dad were squeezing past each other. They were climbing over and around dozens of unpacked boxes.

"Where's my blue denim coat?" Sarah demanded. "Has anybody seen my blue denim coat?"

But no one was paying much attention. Mrs. Martin was hunting for bugs with a flyswatter the size of Kansas. Grandma was reminding everyone that the fire in the toaster had started out as bread. Mr. Martin was doing his best imitation of a handyman as he tried to fix the broken paper-towel rack. And little Jamie was sitting on top of the tallest stack of boxes, quietly munching the last of the Captain Crunch.

At last Nicholas himself came into the room. And by the look on his face it was pretty easy to see that he hadn't quite been able to "rise and shine" that morning.

"Hurry, honey. You don't want to be late for your first day at school," Mom said.

Being late wasn't exactly what Nick had in mind. More like never showing up. With eyes sealed shut, he somehow managed to fumble for the nearest box of cereal and dump it into a bowl.

"Please, God," he was praying, "don't let it be bran."

"There, solid as a rock," Dad said as he gave the paper-towel holder a proud pat.

Nicholas paid little attention. He was thinking about his chances of survival at the new school.

Meanwhile, the dog had hopped up on one of the nearby boxes and started gobbling down somebody's toast.

"Get down from there!" Dad shouted at the dog.

He scampered off. But Sarah, who had her back to the whole thing, spun around to her pet's defense.

"Daddy, why are you always picking on Whatever?"

Her father opened his mouth to explain. But Sarah, who was too busy being a teenager, cut him off. "Honestly, Daddy, you've got to learn to loosen up."

With that she popped the remainder of the dog-chewed toast in her mouth.

Dad started to warn her but caught himself. "You're right, honey," was all he said. "I'll try harder." He caught Nicholas's eye and gave him a little wink. Nick managed to smile back.

The phone began to ring, and Grandma headed off to answer it. Meanwhile, Sarah, in a last-ditch effort, turned to her little sister. "Jamie, have *you* seen my blue denim coat?"

The girl nodded, and Sarah's face lit up.

"You have? Where?"

"I was with you the day you bought it."

The light faded as quickly as it was lit. And, with the

world's longest sigh, Sarah turned back out of the kitchen to continue her search.

Jamie quietly followed.

"Look at the time," Dad said, as he glanced at his watch. "I was supposed to be at the paper by 7:30." He gave Mom a quick peck on the cheek and was out the door with the usual good-byes.

Meanwhile, Sarah was calling for help in her search-and-rescue efforts from the other room. "Mother, *please* . . . MOTHER!"

"Coming!" Mom called as she reached for a paper towel and suddenly wound up with the entire "solid as a rock" towel holder in her hand. She groaned slightly as she headed out of the room.

Now, at last, Nicholas was alone. Now, at last, he could have some peace. Now, at last, he could have some quiet. Or so he thought. . . .

TWO

BREAKFAST ADVENTURES

I tried to adjust my eyes to the darkness around me. But it was of no use. I was going to have to feel my way along the jagged walls around me. I was trying to find the famous Eye of Darryl jewel. I would've said things looked hopeless, but it was so dark in there I couldn't tell how things looked!

Suddenly, the cave rocked violently. Loose stones and boulders fell from above. I darted back and forth, dodging one after another after another—a neat trick in the dark.

Finally things started to settle down. I was beginning to feel kind of pleased with myself, having survived another cave-in. But it wasn't over yet.

I heard a low rumbling from behind. I spun around just in

time to see a huge boulder rolling right toward me! I tried to hurry out of the way, but the walls of the cave were so narrow that there was no place for me to hide. The boulder crashed into me and knocked me to the ground. I hit my head and passed out.

When I awoke I noticed that the cave-in had dislodged just enough rocks from above to allow a small shaft of light to pour into my cramped quarters. I could see!

I could see, all right. I could see my legs were pinned behind my old pal, the boulder. I could see that I had really gotten myself in a fix this time. And for what? A jewel?

Ah, yes . . . the jewel. I had to get that jewel. Lying around the cave wasn't getting it done. So, in one swift move I placed my hands against the rock's bumpy surface and pushed. A loud groan echoed in the cave. The noise continued to grow as I pushed harder and harder. It must have been about two minutes before I realized the groan was coming from me.

All that work, and the boulder hadn't moved an inch. Well, I sort of liked it here anyway. Hang some pictures, maybe some curtains—it wouldn't be so bad.

Yeah, right, and sticking your tongue in a blender only tickles.

I had to find a solution. Or, maybe, a solution was about to find me. Because, once again, the cave began to shake. Only this time it was more gentle—more like vibrations. And, as the boulder began to vibrate, I was able to squirm, wiggle, and inch my legs out from under it. The dust and tiny rocks from above kept falling and bouncing off my head. I couldn't help wondering, Is this what eggs feel like when we salt and pepper them?

At last, I freed my feet and rolled aside . . . just as a huge rock crashed down exactly where my head had been. Nick says I'm hardheaded, but I'm glad I hadn't stuck around to find out.

Slowly the shaking began to stop, and everything was quiet . . . yep, you guessed it, too quiet. I couldn't hear a thing.

I snapped my fingers . . . nothing.

I clapped my hands . . . still nothing.

This was just plain crazy. What kind of place was this, anyway?

Suddenly, I felt a tickle in my ear. I shook my head, and a half cup of dirt, two stones, and a moth named Felix came out of my ears. I could hear again! What a relief to know they had only been plugged. I'd still be able to enjoy listening to myself sing in the shower.

I moved on carefully, my way still dimly lit from the shaft of light above. Up ahead I thought I saw a faint glow. Was it just another light shaft, or could it be the prize I was seeking, the wonderful Eye of Darryl jewel? Who knows? With thoughts like these racing through my mind, I began to worry that maybe those "little" rocks that hit me on the head hadn't been so little after all.

In any case, as I worked my way toward the glow, I began to recall the stories and fables told of the ancient jewel—its incredible beauty and untold worth. Soon it would be mine—all mine! Of course I'd be generous and share it with all the little people who had so feebly tried to help me along the way. . . . Come to think of it, I don't know anybody "littler" than me. Oh well, I guess I'll just have to cope with all that wealth by myself.

By now the glorious glow was just a few yards ahead. This was no shaft of light. This was the moment I had dreamed about!

Closer . . . closer . . . closer . . .

There, at last. It was right in front of me. I could see it clearly now. It was beyond description! It was unlike anything I had dreamed of! It was a . . . a . . . magnifying glass! A magnifying glass? Yeah, it was just a magnifying glass, all right.

So much for legends and fables. Here I had risked my life and limb—and for what? For some cheap little toy that made things look bigger. And now, as I held it up, I realized it made everything look bigger—even my stupidity.

But I had no time to dwell on IQs. Because, just at that moment, I heard scraping and clawing. It was coming from below, and it was making its way toward me . . . loud and fast . . . loud and fast. I figured now was as good a time as any to start picking up my pace. I mean, I didn't want to hang around all day. I had things to do, people to see, and spooky things that climb in caves to run away from! It wasn't that I was scared or anything like that. It's just that it suddenly occurred to me that I might have left my electric train running back at the sketch pad.

So I began to climb . . . fast.

But the faster I climbed, the faster it climbed. The clawing and grunting sounds grew louder by the second. I was concerned about it catching up. Slipping and falling back into the pit to face "The Guardian of the Magnifying Glass" was not my idea of a good time.

I kept climbing as fast as I could. But I knew I couldn't keep up the pace much longer. I was about to blow a lung. Something had to give. And, as fate would have it, something did. . . .

As I placed my foot on a large rock, it gave way beneath me.

I started falling. But at the last second, I managed to grab a small opening in the stony wall. I held on for dear life, expecting the monster to be on top of me any second. But I never saw him. Instead, all I heard was the dull thud of the large rock on what must have been the monster's head. Then I heard the tumbling and bouncing sound as both of them fell into the darkness below.

Moments later I made my way to the opening of the cave, coughing and sputtering from the dust of my adventure.

Much to my surprise, my little buddy, Nick, was there to greet me. And, not wanting to alarm him, I casually lifted my magnifying glass to one eye and calmly exclaimed, "Here's looking at you, kid."

"What are you doing?" he replied.

I figured he was trying not to show his concern.

Now, it's true, the "cave" did look a lot like his breakfast cereal box . . . and, okay, so maybe the magnifying glass was just the prize in that box. But at least he could congratulate me for my great imagination and for a job well done. I mean, I did get the prize.

But I could see he had other things on his mind. Most of them having to do with the move to the new neighborhood . . . and to the new school.

"First day at a new school, huh, kid?" I said.

"Yeah," he mumbled as he took another bite of his cereal.

"Ah, cheer up. It's like I always say," I began as I hopped out of the cereal box and onto the table, "make a big first impression, and the rest is a piece of cake." I have a lot of catchy sayings like that, but it didn't seem to faze ol' Nick. Not today.

"Right, McGee," he said. "Remember the last time you told me to make a big impression?"

"Sure, at the all-school play." I also have a great memory.

"Yeah, you told me to push my way to the front of the stage so everybody could see me."

"Right," I agreed. "You were a smash!"

"Sure, when I fell over the edge into Bobby Rusco's tuba!"

"Well, at least you made an impression," I joked. But Nick wasn't laughing.

Mom called from the other room. "Hurry, Nicholas, or you'll be late for school."

With magnifying glass still in hand, I strolled over to my sketch pad lying on the table. Nicholas called back, "Right, Mom."

Scooping up his backpack, he reached for the pad only to find me posed in my best Sherlock Holmes outfit, peering through my newfound prize. "Nice, huh?" I grinned, hoping it would add a little cheer to his life.

"Grow up," was all he said as he slammed the pad shut.

It was going to be a long day. . . .

THREE

TOUGH TIMES FOR THE NEW KID

School was worse than Nick had imagined. Being the "new kid" was one thing. But being the new kid and looking like a total fool was a whole 'nother ball game—a game that Nicholas had become a star player in by the end of the day.

First there was the matter of finding his room. A simple task, right? The office wrote down the number 19 on a piece of paper and gave it to him. The only problem was they gave it to him upside down. So, as the bell rang and everyone ran to their rooms, poor Nicholas was still searching for room 61 instead of 19. The job was made even tougher since the room numbers only went up to 21.

By the time the tardy bell rang, all the kids had slipped

into their classes. All except Nicholas, that is. Now he was alone in the hall. There was no one to ask for help. Nicholas grew more and more desperate as he kept searching for a room that didn't exist . . . until suddenly, out of nowhere, Coach Slayter appeared.

Now, at last, there was help.

Well, not exactly. If it had been any other teacher except Slayter, Nick would have been right. But it was Slayter, so he was wrong.

The coach was probably an okay guy—down deep inside, *way* down inside, so far down that nobody saw it. Basically, the man only had one problem. It had to do with kids. He hated them. Well, not really *hate*. He just thought that all kids were headed for trouble.

For this reason the kids did everything they could to stay out of his way. It's true, they had to sit through his health class. And it's true, they had to put up with his drill-sergeant-type yelling every Tuesday and Thursday when he came over from the middle school to teach PE. But nobody, *nobody* ever made the mistake of crossing him.

Well, almost nobody . . .

Nicholas swallowed hard as he slowly looked up—past the huge thighs, past the bulging stomach, and finally to the neckless head.

"A little soon to be cutting class, isn't it, mister?"

Nicholas gave a frail grin and tried to swallow. But of course there was nothing to swallow. His mouth was as dry as cotton. And before he could explain that he could not find room 61 . . . before he could explain that he was brand new, Slayter had him by the collar and was dragging him back toward the office. Another troublemaker was busted.

Then there was lunch. . . .

All the kids were hanging around the room, busy being kids—laughing, talking, having a good time. Nick had met a few of them. But most of them were too caught up in their little groups to pay him much attention. That is, until he carried his backpack over to the coatracks and got his lunch. It was a simple procedure, right? I mean anyone could toss his backpack up on the shelf and grab his lunch, right? But not today. Not for Nick. Not the way his luck was running.

He tossed the backpack up on the shelf. But the shelf was a little higher than he thought. The backpack came tumbling back down—right in his face. No biggie. Could happen to anyone. He tossed it up again. Again it fell. And again. And, well, you guessed it. Then he heard it . . . giggling.

He glanced over his shoulder to see two girls. They were sitting at nearby desks and covering their mouths. There were no sounds now. But their bodies were shaking, and their eyes crinkling. It was a safe guess that they were the ones who had been enjoying his show.

Nick recognized the one girl right away. She was wearing a silver bow in her hair. *It looks like something from my Erector set*, Nick had thought while staring at it a few classes earlier. The rest of her outfit was equally weird. A bright pink coat with big black spots. Zebra sunglasses that she twirled around and around in her hand. And a zillion bracelets that clanged and tinkled every time she moved—something she did a lot of.

Nicholas felt the edges of his ears start to burn. He wasn't used to being such a moron. He tried to cover up by giving the girls a weak little smile. Then, one last time, he gave the backpack a mighty heave. Finally, *finally* it stayed put. Success!

He looked back to the girls and gave a little chuckle as he reached for his sack lunch. Now he was in control. Now he could laugh at himself with the best of them. After all, he was definitely not the clumsy fool they thought they were watching. He knew it. And now, by laughing at himself, they knew he knew it.

But in his cool hipness, Nicholas grabbed his lunch sack by the wrong end. And, as he pulled it off the shelf, everything spilled out of the top . . . everything—his bologna sandwich, his Fritos, his Oreos, and his apple . . . which started rolling across the room.

The rest of the kids stopped talking and turned to watch the apple as it continued to roll. In the new silence it sounded like thunder. Finally, one person started to clap. Another followed, and another, until the whole room was clapping . . . and laughing. Nicholas wasn't sure what to do. But the smile had worked before so he tried it again.

So there he was, trying to look like a good sport by wearing the stupidest grin he had ever worn in his life. His lunch lay all over the ground at his feet. Yes sirree, if there were any doubts before, he put them all to rest. He definitely looked like the class idiot now.

Then there was recess. . . .

Nicholas had been trying to decide whether or not he should go back into the classroom and get his sketch pad. Things had been pretty rough. To do a little drawing right now might cheer him up. Maybe he could even have a little chat with McGee. But that last thought made him nervous. All he needed was for McGee to get out of hand and start acting up.

But Nicholas didn't need McGee to get him in trouble. Not just yet. Because, suddenly, he heard a whistle blow and a familiar voice yell out, "Hey, you kids, come back here!"

Three kids rounded the corner of the building and ran head on into Nicholas. These guys were definitely in a hurry—no greetings, no apologies, not even a curse or two for him getting in their way. Instead, as they untangled themselves, each shoved a small can of something into Nicholas's hands and was off.

Nicholas looked down at the cans he was now holding. They were different colors of spray paint. He thought it was odd that the boys would give him such things. That is, until he finished rounding the corner and saw Coach Slayter with the whistle in his hand. The coach was not smiling.

For a moment Nick was confused . . . until he noticed the picture of the coach freshly painted on the wall beside the man.

Nicholas looked to the cans in his hands, then up to the coach.

He tried to smile.

Once again, Slayter grabbed him by the collar. Once again, the two were heading for the office.

Bang! Clittery-clank-clank-clitter.

It wasn't the toughest day Nicholas ever had.

Bang! Clank, clitter-clitter-clitter.

But at that moment he couldn't think of any that had been tougher.

Bang! Clittery-clittery-clank.

"Make an impression," McGee had said. "Let everyone know who you are."

Well, he had certainly done that. It's pretty hard to sit in the principal's office for half an hour writing "I will respect public property" a billion times. It's pretty hard to sit there as every teacher in school comes to check their box and looks down at you thinking, *Hmmm, another tough kid. Better keep my eye on him.* It's pretty hard to do all that and *not* make an impression.

Bang! Clittery-clank-clank-clitter.

Now, he was walking down an alley. A poor tomato juice can, whose label had worn off blocks ago, was taking the brunt of all his anger.

What else could possibly go wrong?

Bang! Clittery-clank-clank . . . THUD.

He looked up.

Ahead of him were four boys standing in a circle. Citizens of the Month they were not. Long hair, pierced ears, dark sweatshirts. Let's just say they were the type of kids Coach

Slayter hated. And, speaking of Slayter, suddenly it wouldn't have been so bad to have him around again. In fact, right now Nicholas wouldn't even have minded being in trouble again—especially as he looked helplessly at the four gang members glaring at him.

And the reason for the glare?

Nicholas's can was leaning against one of their skateboards.

"What do you think you're doin'?" the tallest member asked. His voice sounded hoarse and grave, like he'd just been munching on rocks. He probably had.

"Me?" Nicholas said. It was a stupid response, but he couldn't think of anything smarter.

"Come here."

Nick hesitated but decided to obey—or at least his feet did. Getting closer to the gang was not what the rest of his body had in mind.

"Look at my skateboard," the thug said as he picked up the road-worn board. It was plastered from head to toe with heavy-metal decals. "You almost put a nick in it. What's your name?"

"Nick."

"Yeah, right, that's what I'm talkin' 'bout. Now what's your name, kid?"

"Uh . . . Nick."

A couple of the gang members snickered. The leader threw them a look. Turning back to Nicholas, he grabbed the boy's shirt and pulled him in. "Oh, you're a funny man. A regular—"

Finally Nicholas caught on and quickly blurted out, "Nicholas . . . my name is Nicholas!"

The leader relaxed slightly. Apparently this new kid wasn't trying to be a smart aleck. He was just stupid.

"Okay, St. Nicholas," the leader growled as the tiniest trace of a smile—or was it a sneer?—crossed his lips. "You got a present for me?"

"What?" Nick asked.

The anger started to return to the leader's voice. "If you come down my alley throwing cans at me, you had better have some kind of a peace offering."

Nicholas couldn't have been more lost. Getting a broken face was not his idea of a good time, but he had no idea what the leader was talking about.

"Money, stupid."

Glancing down and seeing the leader's right hand tightening into a fist, Nicholas knew two things. One, he had no money. And, two, that was the last answer in the world the kid wanted to hear.

"Well . . . I . . . uh," he stammered.

"Man, you're one lucky dude, kid."

The voice came from behind. Nicholas glanced out the corner of his eye for a better view.

"Beat it, Louis," the leader ordered.

But the kid kept approaching. He was Nicholas's age, and about half the leader's size.

"Sure, man, but I just want him to realize what an honor it is to be beaten up by somebody like you."

Being honored was not exactly how Nicholas saw the situation—but he was grateful for any delay.

Louis continued, this time talking directly to Nick about the leader. "I bet you don't even know that this guy is the roughest, baddest dude in the whole neighborhood. I mean he normally stomps guys twice your size."

Somehow, Nicholas didn't find that fact too comforting.

"But he's willing to risk his reputation by beating up somebody as wimpy as you. I mean my little sister could beat you up." He turned to the leader. "Ain't that right, Derrick?"

Derrick hesitated, unsure about how to respond.

"Go ahead," Louis encouraged. "Smash his face in."

Things were getting pretty muddy in the leader's mind. But smashing faces was one thing he understood. So, raising his fist, he prepared to do just that.

Nicholas closed his eyes, waiting for the worst. But, Louis wasn't finished. "I mean, people aren't going to fear him like they used to. His reputation will never be the same. But Derrick Cryder, a man of principle, is going to sacrifice all that on a little nothing like you."

Louis's logic began to make some kind of strange sense—at least to Derrick. And, after another moment of thought, the leader let Nicholas go with a shove. "Don't you wish," he said. But with the threat of bodily injury still very much on his mind, he growled, "I'm not going to forget you, kid. You either, Louis."

And with that, he turned and left. The rest of the gang followed.

"Hey, I'm your man," Louis called after him.

Now the two boys stood in silence for a moment. Nick's head was reeling over the slickness he had just seen. Talk about smooth. This kid was a work of art. In just two short minutes the little guy had turned the whole slug-fest around. Not only had he saved Nick's face, but he even managed to protect his own. All this without raising a fist. Incredible.

"Thanks, uh . . ." Nicholas was searching for his name.

"Louis," the boy said. And shrugging he added, "Forget it, man."

With that the two turned and started down the alley. Neither knew it then, but a friendship was definitely in the making.

But the day's adventures were not over yet. Not by a long shot. . . .

FOUR

THE CRAZY OLD MAN

Nicholas and Louis came around the corner and started up the street. Nick said good-bye to the boy and turned to cut across the neighbor's yard. He just lived a block over. By crossing through the driveway and into the next alley he'd be home in seconds.

But not this time.

"What are you doing?" Louis called.

A little taken by his tone, Nicholas stuttered, "I, uh, I was going home."

"Not that way you don't."

"Sure, I just live over on the other side . . ."

"Man, what are you thinking? No one cuts across *that* yard."

"Why not?" Nicholas asked as he turned to look at the house. Now it's true, the house *did* seem a little spooky—three stories tall, broken shutters, pitch black windows, sagging roof. All right, it looked a *lot* spooky.

"He's a crazy old man. He eats live animals. They say anything that goes into that yard don't come out again!"

Nicholas could only stare. "What do you mean? Like pets and stuff?"

"Anything."

Enough said. Nick already had had enough adventure for the day—or even for the whole year. No way did he want to be eaten alive by some crazy man. But as he turned back to join Louis, he felt a sudden movement inside the art pad he was carrying. . . .

"Psst, Nick . . . Nick!" I was whispering, trying not to let Louis overhear. This was a perfect situation. I didn't want my little buddy to blow it. The day had been tough. He obviously wasn't thinking too clearly. Otherwise he would have known how close we were to turning it all around.

"Where have you been?" Nick whispered back.

"Never mind that. . . . This is your chance!"

He just looked at me.

"To make that big impression!" I explained.

I guess Nick was a little spooked by the old place. That meant that I would have to take command.

"Look, Nick, just go up and tap on one of those windows. We'll be heroes."

Still no response.

"C'mon, Nick. Don't blow this one. Louis is already watching, so let's just give him something to look at."

Nick looked at the house, then at me, then back to the house. All my talk was obviously doing some good. If he just knocked on one of the windows, the news of his courage would quickly spread. No longer would he be "Nicholas the Klutz" or "Nicholas the Hood." Now he could be "Nicholas the Macho." I could see it in his eyes. It all started to make sense to him.

I clucked like a chicken—just to remind him what he'd be if he didn't go. "C'mon, kid. I'll be with you all the way."

He took a deep breath and ran for the closest window—the one right above the cellar doors. I let go with one of my great battle cries. "TIPPY-CANOE, I'M WITH YOU!" We were off. . . .

In a flash Nicholas was up on the cellar doors and stretching for all he was worth to tap on the window.

This is going to be easier than I thought . . . before I heard the sound of cracking wood under our feet. All of a sudden the ground was missing!

We fell through the broken doors and tumbled down the cellar steps like clowns in the circus. But there was no applause. Instead, we heard all kinds of screeching, clawing, and squawking!

It took a moment for our eyes to adjust to the darkness. But when they did, we saw cages filled with all sorts of things that screamed and growled and gurgled.

During the fall Nicholas had dropped my sketch pad, and for the moment I was trapped under it. But, not being one to panic, I calmly said, "LET'S GET OUT OF HERE!"

It did the trick. Nicholas scrambled to his feet. Unfortunately, he found himself standing face to face with large, growling teeth . . . attached to an even larger bobcat!

He let out a scream and threw himself back over a stack of wooden crates. I'd seen this kind of behavior before. I had to get him under control. I had to snap him out of it. I had to stop my teeth from chattering long enough so I could speak!

Outside, I could hear the faint sound of Louis screaming, "Get out of there, Nick. Get out of there!"

Nicholas scampered back to his feet and was ready to escape. But, before he could move, a shaft of light pierced the darkness. It came from the top of the stairs leading into the man's house. A huge, dark figure appeared at the door. I tried to shout, to scream, but nothing came out.

The figure drew closer and closer. His shadow was now pouring across our faces. He was nearly on top of us.

"Nicholas!" I finally managed to squeak. "RUN!"

Nick snapped out of his trance and began looking for an escape. I was proud of the kid. With the right coaching, he could do almost anything. But what about me? I was still pinned underneath the sketch pad!

"Nicholas . . . don't leave me here!"

He jumped back and scooped up my pad . . . while I hung on for dear life.

But as he straightened up he came nose to nose with a rabbit. That's right, a poor, defenseless rabbit. The helpless animal was hanging from the man's huge hand—probably his idea of an afternoon snack.

Nicholas let out a scream, tore past the big man, and raced up the stairs toward the light. We were across the dimly lit room and out the front door in a flash.

We were going so fast that we hardly noticed running right into Louis on the sidewalk in front of the house. I guess he'd been waiting for our bones to be thrown out after we were eaten. We continued at lightning speed until we were safely in Nick's room—or, rather, in his closet.

FIVE

THE LIE BEGINS

Nicholas's head was spinning. He had just finished dinner but didn't know what he ate. His mind was too busy thinking. It's a pity, too. Because from what he could tell by the remains of the pork chops and Rice-A-Roni, it had been one of his favorite meals. Oh, well, maybe next time.

Of course his folks asked the usual first-day-at-school questions: How did he like his teacher? How were the kids? Was he making friends? You know, the usual stuff.

And, of course, Nicholas gave the usual eleven-year-old answers: Fine. Okay. I guess.

It's not that he didn't want to talk to his parents. He loved talking to them. And they loved listening. No matter how busy they were, Mom and Dad always made it a point to talk with their kids.

But today he didn't feel like talking. Today, with all that Nicholas had gone through . . . well, he just wasn't sure where to start. So he wouldn't start at all. For now, the "fines," "okays," and shrugging shoulders would just have to do.

Both parents noticed his silence. But neither of them forced him to talk. They knew he was upset about something—but they also knew they couldn't push. He would say more when he was ready.

And they were right. He would.

But now his mind was racing a billion miles an hour. It was racing about the man he'd run into. It was racing about Derrick. And it was racing about his rotten day at school.

It was racing when he finally got to sleep. . . . And it was still racing when he woke up the next morning and got ready for school.

After putting up with the usual good-byes and pecks on the cheek, Nicholas grabbed his stuff and headed for the door. As he opened it he couldn't help thinking, *At least today will be better than yesterday.*

But then he saw Louis. . . .

"There he is now—the man that knows no fear," Louis said. He had gathered a couple of his friends together. They had been waiting outside Nicholas's house. For how long, Nick didn't know.

"Did you get a look at him?" Louis asked.

For a moment Nick didn't know what he was talking about.

"The man, the crazy guy—was he big?"

"Uh," Nicholas said. "Well, yeah, he . . ."

"I knew it!" Louis interrupted. "Like a monster, wasn't he?"

Again Nick was caught a little off guard. What did Louis mean by "monster"? And why were the other kids there? And why . . . ? Then he saw it: The look on Louis's face. The boy was eager for a story. And the bigger it was the better it would be.

Nicholas wasn't sure what to do. He really didn't want to disappoint Louis—not after he brought all his friends.

But, at the same time, he really didn't want to lie.

So Nicholas did the next best thing. He just didn't *dis*agree. "Well, he was, uh . . ."

Louis took the bait. "I told you," he said to his friends. Then, back to Nicholas, "Were there any animals?"

"Oh, yeah, there were animals every—"

"I knew it! Did you see him eating any?"

Things were closing in on Nicholas. Up until now he didn't have to officially lie. But wasn't agreeing with a lie just as bad as telling one? And look at those kids' faces. They were so eager for a hero. Besides, all day yesterday Nick had been a real goon. And now there was a way to regain some respect!

"Well, uh," Nicholas said, hesitating. "He had a rabbit."

"He had a rabbit? He was eating a rabbit?"

More hesitating. "Well, it was still alive."

"He was eating a *LIVE* rabbit?!"

Uh-oh. Here it was. All Nicholas had to do was say yes. Just one little "white" lie. Who would know? Who would care? "Well, uh, I guess . . . ," he said, stalling.

The kids continued to stare. How could he let them down? How could he let himself down? Besides, after all he went through yesterday, he needed it. He deserved it.

"Yeah, yeah," he heard himself saying. "It was alive." And then, almost before he could catch himself, the words spilled out. "Whatever was left of it."

There, he had done it.

"This is great, man!" Louis looked like he was going to explode. "This is great!" He started running, and the other kids followed him. "Wait until they hear this. This is great!"

Nicholas waited. Part of him felt pretty good about what had happened. He was feeling good about the excitement he had caused. He was feeling good about being the center of it. After all, *he* had been there. *He* was the expert. *He* was the one who had met this terrible "monster" face-to-face and lived to talk about it. So why shouldn't he enjoy a little glory?

But still, somewhere past the "good feelings," he felt a little guilt. Somewhere, even deeper, he knew it was wrong.

But who would know?

Who would care?

News spread faster than Nicholas could have imagined. Not only did it spread faster, it spread bigger.

In fact, by the time they got off the bus at school, he could see Louis's arms flying wildly. He was making all kinds of faces. Nicholas couldn't hear what was being said, but he did manage to catch a phrase or two about "huge claws" and "trying to catch the new kid."

That little guilt Nicholas had felt before was starting to grow.

It grew as he noticed more and more kids looking at him during class. It grew when kids stopped talking as soon as he came near. And it grew when complete strangers (usually girls) began passing and saying, "Hi."

But Nicholas noticed it the most when he was heading back from the lunchroom. Not far away, the girl with the Erector-set hair bow was telling a crowd something about "long pointed fangs that were dripping—" But she never finished. When she saw Nicholas, she stopped and pointed. "There he is now!"

Everyone in the group turned to stare.

Nicholas came to a stop. He didn't know what to do with ten people staring at him.

He gave a weak idiotic smile (the one he had become so good at the day before).

They continued to stare.

He knew he had to say something. He knew he had to make some sort of speech. So, he opened his mouth and said, "Hi."

"Hi," they all said back.

Again he smiled. Being famous was tough.

They continued to stare.

He could feel his ears burning again. He glanced around and swallowed hard. Then he started toward the building.

The group didn't say a word. They just continued to stare.

He could feel them staring at his back as he bumped into a couple of kids near the doorway and finally stumbled inside.

Now he was out of sight. Now he could breathe.

But he didn't stop walking. He headed down the hall toward his classroom as quickly as possible. He could sit down there. At least for a little while, he could stay out of sight.

Now that doesn't mean Nicholas didn't enjoy the fame. To be honest, he thought it was great. But as the day went on, that "greatness" started to wear off. Instead, the good feelings started being replaced more and more by the other feeling—by that guilt.

Two-thirty had never come slower. Over and over again Nicholas looked to the clock. Over and over again he tried to make the hands move forward just by thinking. If the bell would just ring. If the day would just hurry up and end. By tomorrow everyone would forget about him and the man with the animals. By tomorrow they would find something new to talk about.

But that was tomorrow. Today was still today. And, at the moment, it didn't look like today would ever finish.

Mrs. Sanford, his teacher, was talking on and on about fractions and decimals. She kept talking and talking and talking. Then, when she was through, she talked some more. Nick kept looking at the clock. It wouldn't budge. He was beginning to believe that somehow he had managed to stumble into an episode of *The Twilight Zone* where time was always and forever frozen at 2:29.

Then it happened. The clock clicked that quarter of an inch, the bell rang, and everybody flew out of their seats.

Now, at last, he could head for home. Now, at last, he could forget about this day.

He grabbed his coat and backpack and headed out the door, free at last—until Derrick stepped in his path.

"Hey, kid. So you're some big hero now."

Nick swallowed hard, hoping the boy wouldn't ask him to prove it.

Just then a couple of girls passed. "Hello, Nicholas."

For a second Nick was pleased. But only for a second.

"Well, I ain't buying this hero stuff," Derrick growled. "I mean what kind of fool do you take me for?"

"How many kinds are there?"

Nicholas immediately hated himself for trying to be funny with so few seconds left in his life.

But Derrick didn't laugh. He didn't get mad either. In fact, for a moment it looked as if he were actually trying to figure out the answer. But the question was too tough for him, so he finally continued. "Don't try to change the subject," he said.

Kids were starting to gather around.

"If this crazy, drooling man is supposed to be such a monster, eating all these pets and stuff," Derrick demanded, "then where'd you get the guts to stand up to him?"

Nicholas wasn't sure what to say. Luckily he didn't have to worry about it. Before he could open his mouth, the girl with the metal bow spoke up.

"What do you know about guts, Derrick? You're scared to even go near the place."

Nicholas could see the veins in the boy's neck jump and stand out. He could see the muscles in his jaw tighten. Finally Derrick spoke. But it wasn't loud and it wasn't boasting. It was more frightening than that. It was quiet.

And Nicholas could tell he meant every word of it.

"That old man is as good as dead."

SIX

THE PLOT SICKENS

Nicholas doesn't remember how he got home that day. He's sure he got there eventually. And he's sure of another thing. He didn't cut through his neighbor's yard. But the exact route? Well, Nick had too many other things on his mind to pay attention to those sorts of details.

He was thinking about the whole mess. Maybe that man deserved whatever Derrick was going to do to him. After all, he was the one with the spooky, run-down house. And he was the one who caught all those poor animals and kept them locked up in cages. Maybe it was time for a little justice.

Yet, Nicholas knew that Derrick Cryder was not the right

one to see that justice was done. The thought made Nick more than a little nervous.

But you couldn't blame Nick. His was just a little white lie. It wasn't his fault things had gotten so out of hand. It wasn't his fault everybody kept making the story bigger. It wasn't his fault they planned to do something to the crazy man.

Or was it?

Around and around Nicholas's thoughts went until finally he arrived at home.

"Shameful, just shameful," Grandma was saying to Nick's mom as he opened the door. Grandma was at the kitchen sink cleaning lettuce. Mom was at the table snapping beans. Nicholas entered the room and made a beeline for the refrigerator.

"Hi, hon, how was school?" Mom asked.

"All right." Nick shrugged. He looked around for something to eat. He was back to his shrugs and one-word answers.

"What exactly happened?" he heard his mother ask his grandma.

"Seems some child broke into George Ravenhill's cellar yesterday—scared the poor man half to death."

Nicholas slowly came to a stop. Were they talking about him? After all, *he* had fallen through somebody's cellar yesterday.

"Is that the place," Mom asked, "a block away that's so run down?"

"Yes, it is run down," Grandma agreed. "But with his aching bones, that poor old man can barely move about."

Nicholas could feel a small knot in his stomach. They *were* talking about him *and* the crazy man. He closed the refrigerator door empty handed. Suddenly eating was the last thing he wanted to do.

Grandma continued. "Such a sweet soul, too. He takes care of all those poor injured animals."

The knot tightened.

"I don't care what his house looks like. He's the nicest man you'd ever want to meet."

More was said, but Nicholas didn't hear it. All he knew was that everything the kids said and believed about that "crazy" man was wrong. Dead wrong. The house was run down because the man was crippled and couldn't keep it fixed up. The animals were in cages because he was taking care of them. And, most important, he was not some mean, cruel monster. He was a kind man doing his best to help others. "A sweet soul," Grandma had called him.

That knot in Nicholas's stomach continued to tighten.

He was not interested in eating now . . . and he would not be able to eat dinner later.

Nick managed to climb the stairs to his room. He closed the door and lay on his bed looking around.

At school Nick tended to be pretty quiet and shy. But you wouldn't know it by his room. It was anything but normal. All of the imagination he kept pent up when he was outside exploded when he came inside. It exploded on every wall, every shelf, every piece of furniture, the ceiling, the floor, you name it.

An automatic peanut cracker here.

A remote control pencil sharpener there.

A live goldfish swimming inside a gumball machine.

A stegosaurus lurking in the corner.

A cowboy riding a spaceship.

Even a mini-jukebox that flashed "Nick's Café, Nick's Café, Nick's Café."

And he had only moved in a few days ago! But he had plans for turning it into a great museum full of all sorts of gizmos, widgets, and whatchamacallits. Already he had plans for

An automatic bubble blower made from an old fan, a
    mannequin's head, Groucho Marx glasses, and parts
    of a toy lawn mower.

A voice-activated light switch.

An alarm activated by a flying puppet, a crashing jet
    fighter, and a swinging boxing glove.

And a robot arm attached to the ceiling that would
    automatically reach down and make his bed.

Of course these were all future projects. But it didn't hurt too much to dream. And dreaming was something Nicholas knew how to do.

Then there was his drawing table . . .

Nicholas and McGee spent hours and hours here as the boy drew one adventure after another. Of course, McGee always wanted to be the hero in the stories, and Nick usually let him. But Nicholas was the one with the power. He was the one with the pencil. And, if McGee got too out of hand, Nicholas was also the one with the eraser.

But Nick wasn't sitting at his table now. Nor was he dreaming about his room. Instead, he sat on the bed and quietly drew on his sketch pad. He wasn't sure what it would be. But it slowly began looking like the face of a man.

There was a gentle tap at his door. It didn't surprise Nicholas. Getting permission to miss dinner was a major event. He knew his folks would be concerned. And he knew they'd eventually come up and talk. They were like that. And even though it was sometimes a pain, deep down inside Nicholas was glad for their concern.

He reached for his flashlight and directed its beam across the room to a toy radar dish. The dish began to swivel back and forth, switching the Don't Walk sign to Walk. This triggered a miniature globe to spin above the door, which released a large sword. The sword fell, activating a series of weights and pulleys that opened the door.

Now it's true, it would have been a lot easier to just get up and open the door. But it wouldn't be nearly as inventive . . . or as much fun.

"Can I come in?" Dad poked his head around the door.

Nick nodded.

His dad entered and glanced about the room. "Sure fixed this place up in a hurry," he commented.

It was true, and Nicholas was pleased his dad noticed. But for now he just shrugged it off.

"Missed you at dinner."

More silence. The boy knew what his father was doing. The man wanted to talk. But Nicholas didn't know what to say. Part of him wanted Dad to stick around. The other part wanted him to go away.

Dad sensed the confusion. So, instead of pushing and asking a lot of hard questions, he just quietly walked over to the other end of the room. "You know, living here with Grandma is going to be great. I've got a lot of memories about this old place."

To be honest, Nicholas felt he'd already had enough memories.

"It was right over there your Uncle Rob 'accidentally' shoved me into the dresser and chipped this tooth. Oh, how I cried. I almost got him thrown in jail." Dad smiled at the memory.

Nicholas tried to join in with a smile of his own. But he didn't have much success.

More silence.

Finally Dad strolled over to the foot of the bed and sat. Then, after a long moment, he spoke. "What's up, Nick?"

"About what?" The words were out of the boy's mouth before he could stop them. But they did no good. He knew that his dad knew. Maybe not the details, but they'd been friends too many years for him to be able to hide something this important.

Finally, Nicholas answered. "I don't know." He stalled, giving his dad one last chance to give up and leave. But his dad had all the time in the world. He wasn't going anywhere, and Nicholas knew it.

Finally, seeing no way out, Nick began. "What if—what if you said something about somebody and, you know, they got in real trouble for it?"

A trace of relief started to cross his dad's face. "Well, Son, nobody likes to get somebody in trouble. But if it's the truth and—"

Nicholas's eyes shot down.

Dad didn't miss it.

"Of course," he continued gently, "if it's not the truth . . ."

Nicholas didn't say a word.

His dad finally saw the picture. His son had lied. With that information he quietly continued. "Then a lot of people could get hurt."

Nicholas still didn't look up. But that was okay. He didn't need to. Dad knew what was going on in his mind and he wanted to help. So he gently went on. "Of course, there's the person that's being lied about. But there's also the person who's doing the lying."

Nick looked up. It's true, *he* was hurting. Sure, he may have caused that old man some problems. But he, Nicholas Martin, was also hurting—more than he thought possible.

Dad continued. "I mean, not only will the truth eventually find the liar out, but the very fact that lying is a sin—well, that sin starts cutting off that person's friendship with God."

Of course! That's what he'd been feeling! The knot in his stomach, that feeling. Sure it felt great to be the hero, to have everyone think you were a hotshot. But that other feeling—that feeling of guilt. That's what it was. It was cutting off his friendship with God, with Jesus. It was sin. Plain and simple. And it hurt.

Still, Dad was not finished. "But you know there's a third person that gets hurt."

A frown crossed Nicholas's face. There was more? Wasn't the pain and ache enough?

"Yes," Dad continued, "there is one more person who gets hurt."

Nicholas waited.

"Remember, Jesus said that whatever we do for others we do for him."

Nicholas nodded. He remembered hearing something like that in Sunday school.

"Well, that being the case, it stands to reason that whatever we do *to* others we do *to* him. If you lie and hurt another person, you're actually lying to Jesus and hurting him."

Nicholas was stunned. He had no idea that such a little lie could cause such big problems. But his dad was right. He could see it clearly now. Not only was he hurting himself, he was also hurting Jesus. Everything he said, everything he did against that man was also against Jesus.

The knot in his stomach was very painful. And now he could also feel a lump in his throat. This isn't what he wanted. He just wanted the kids to like him, to look up to him. He didn't want this. But how could he stop it? How could he fix it?

He tried to speak. His voice was thick and raspy, barely above a whisper. "What do I do?"

His dad waited a long moment as Nicholas looked to him for help. Finally, his father spoke. It wasn't a mean answer. But it wasn't a simple answer either. Instead, he asked just one question: "What do you think?"

SEVEN

THE ATTACK

The alley was dark and full of shadows. There were a few back porch lights on. But the fog was so thick that the lights barely shone. Everything was very, very still. Dark and still. Then a porch light flickered on, lighting the face of Derrick Cryder. He quickly moved back into the shadows and continued to wait.

Nicholas was in his room sketching again. His dad had left several minutes before. Now all he could do was sketch and think. What his dad said kept echoing inside his mind. *"Whatever you do to others, you're doing to Jesus."*

    The drawing was definitely taking on the face of a person.

Nicholas was shading in the nose now. It was a strong nose, a noble nose.

Derrick was standing along the wire fence. He blew into his hands and stomped his feet slightly. The fog had brought a chill to the night.

There was the scratch of gravel off in the distance. He spun around just in time to see one of his fellow gang members appear.

"Hey, man, what's happening?" he whispered. "Soon as the others show up, let's get rolling."

They huddled together just out of the light. And they continued to wait.

Nicholas was working on the chin now. Like the nose, it was going to be a strong chin. *Whisk, whisk, whisk*—his pencil seemed to be moving faster than normal as he continued shading. And Nicholas's own face? The boy had never been in such deep thought. And he still continued to draw.

"All right, there they are!" Derrick whispered.

Two other kids appeared in the alley. Big kids. Kids looking for trouble. They arrived and exchanged hand slaps and more street jive.

"All right. Let's do it to it!"

"Yeah."

"Let's show that crazy old man!" *BANG.* Derrick slammed the wire fence hard, causing it to rattle. A distant dog started barking, followed by another. But that didn't matter. Derrick and the guys were moving out. Derrick and the guys were ready for action.

They started down the alley. Four of them. Their faces appearing and disappearing in the shadows. No one said a word. No one had to. They knew what they had to do, and nothing would stop them.

Now Nicholas was working on the eyes. They were thoughtful eyes, haunting eyes. Eyes full of pain. Eyes full of sorrow. In fact, if you were to have looked into Nicholas's own eyes at that exact moment you would have seen the very same look—thoughtful, painful, sorrowful. The boy was not crying, not yet. But, like the sketch, he was definitely aching.

He hesitated a moment. The eyes were finished. So was the nose, the chin, the hair. But something was missing. Something still was not right. Then he saw it. In a flash he took the pencil and made a fierce, strong line across the forehead. And then another in the opposite direction. For a moment it looked like he had made a giant X across the top of the head. But he was not finished. He made another slash, and one across it, making another X. And then another.

His eyes began to fill with tears. He angrily brushed them aside and continued to draw.

Derrick and his gang came out of the alley and into the bright streetlights. They didn't care if anyone saw them now. They no longer needed the darkness. There were four of them, and four could do just about whatever they wanted.

The old man's house was just ahead.

Derrick scooped up a large rock. His buddies did likewise. And, after a few more steps, they were in front of the house.

There was only one light on. It was downstairs. But it was good enough.

Derrick leaned back and let his rock fly. . . .

It was a quiet evening inside George Ravenhill's living room. He had put on some gentle music and was enjoying the fire in the fireplace. For several hours he had been hovering over the worktable. That afternoon a young cardinal had flown into one of the neighbor's picture windows. The neighbor had brought it over, and Ravenhill was doing all he could to save it. At the moment he was trying to feed it some sugar water with an eyedropper with his crippled hands. At last he succeeded.

Suddenly, there was a loud crash!

Ravenhill spun around just in time to see the rock fly into the room. It was followed by a thousand bits of glass. He covered his eyes with his arm just in time as the glass sprayed over him.

There was laughter outside, but he didn't have time to see who it was.

Another rock came crashing through the window, followed by more glass. Quickly, he grabbed a nearby towel and threw it over the cardinal. Glass was flying in all directions, but he was more concerned about the bird's safety than his own. There was one more crash, and then all was silent.

Well, not really silent. Outside on the porch, some of the other caged animals he was taking care of were scared—dogs, birds, kittens, his pet rabbit, even a raccoon. They were barking, and screaming, and crying.

Ravenhill was also frightened. He lay huddled on the floor shaking like a leaf. What had he done? Why were people trying to hurt him?

Time passed slowly, but there were no more rocks. Finally he rose to his feet and hobbled across the broken glass to stand beside the shattered window. After a deep breath, he pushed the curtains aside to look out. But there was no sign of movement. Everything was quiet again.

Except for the animals. They were still very frightened, and it would take a long time to quiet them down. But the animals were not the only ones afraid.

George Ravenhill would not be able to sleep that night.

Nor would Nicholas. Oh, he was in his bed all right. His eyes were shut. In fact, he even managed to doze off once in a while. But each time he fell asleep the dreams would come. Bad dreams. Scary dreams. Sometimes there were monsters, sometimes demons. Sometimes he was just falling and falling and falling. But each and every time he would wake from them with a start. And, after convincing himself that it was just a dream, he would close his eyes and drift back off to sleep. But it would be only for a few minutes. Another dream would soon be coming.

Not far away was the picture Nick had been drawing. It was finished now. And now, with its noble nose, strong chin, and deep, sorrowful eyes, there was no missing who it was. It was a portrait of Jesus.

But this was not a smiling Jesus. This was not the happy Jesus with arms reaching out that Nick always saw at Sunday school. This was a different Jesus. This was a Jesus who was hurting.

And on top of his head were the *Xs* Nicholas had drawn. But they were not just *Xs*. Strung together they had become a crown of thorns. The crown of thorns Jesus had been forced to wear. The crown of thorns the soldiers had jammed down hard on his head until it bled. The crown of thorns he had worn as he died on the cross for all of our sins.

"Whatever you do to others, you're doing to Jesus."

EIGHT

A TIME FOR ACTION

Nicholas was right—and he was wrong.

He was right when he figured the kids at school would forget about him by the next day. It's true, he was no longer in the spotlight. They were treating him just like your average kid.

But he was wrong when he thought they'd forget about the old man. Derrick saw to that. Now Derrick was the one with all the courage. He was the one who attacked the house. He was the one who actually stood up to the "monster." Nick may have fallen through his cellar doors. But Derrick was the one who taught the man a lesson. Derrick Cryder was the hero for today.

And Derrick played it for all it was worth.

He played it at recess when the shy girls looked at him—or when the bolder ones actually came up and flirted.

He played it at lunchtime when the guys came up and slapped him on the back.

He was enjoying the attention so much that he didn't want it to end. So by the end of the day, he was making new plans. He was going to continue being the hero. "Trash the Crazy Man's House—Part 2" was about to begin.

But Nicholas didn't know that. Not yet. And that was probably good. You see, the day had been rough enough on him as it was. Because each time he heard what Derrick had done, a pain shot through him—that pain in his stomach.

It's true that Nicholas was not the one who broke the windows. But a part of him felt as though he was the one. Derrick may have thrown the rocks, but Nicholas was the one who had let the rumors grow. And Nick was the one who had stood by and let everyone believe them.

Nicholas was sitting in math class when the 2:30 bell rang to signal the end of the day. Everyone sprang into action. They began packing up their backpacks and grabbing their coats. They began heading for home. But Nicholas stayed behind at his desk. He was drawing some little design on his sketch pad when Louis suddenly popped his head into the room.

"Hey, Nick! If you don't move it, you're going to miss the action!"

"What action?" Nick asked.

"Derrick and his friends are going to put the finishing touches on the old man!"

Nick couldn't believe his ears. They were going back. They were going back to Mr. Ravenhill's to do more damage!

Louis flashed him a grin. "Should be good," he said. And he was out the door.

Now Nicholas was all alone.

What should he do?

What could he do?

This was a time for Major Mishap to spring into action! Not only for the sake of poor Mr. Ravenhill but also for my little pal, Nick. He just didn't know what to do. So, dashing into a nearby sketchpad, I changed into my superhero clothes. I leaped from the pad in Nick's backpack and out onto the top of his desk.

"This is it, loyal friend," I declared, as my cape blew behind me in the wind.

"McGee, please, not Major Mishap again."

Nick sounded a bit upset. Now, most wrongdoers respond that way when Major Mishap arrives on the scene. But it seemed a bit strange coming from my own partner. Now I admit some of my adventures haven't always come out exactly perfect, but this was no time to be picky about the past. . . .

"It's time to right the wrongs, to restore justice to its rightful place, to—"

"McGee," he interrupted. "If I try to stop those guys they'll kill me!"

Over the years Nick and I have been through a lot together.

And, although most of our times are fun and games, I know when he's hurting. And this . . . well, this was one of those times. We looked at each other for a long moment, searching for an answer. And then, quietly, I said what we both knew.

"There isn't much time, kid."

His lips tightened for a second. Then suddenly, without a word, he jumped to his feet. Grabbing his jacket with one hand, he snatched up the backpack with the other—so quickly that I barely had time to leap back inside.

He wheeled toward the exit and raced out the door.

We were on our way to George Ravenhill's to save the day . . . or die trying.

The balloon exploded against the side of Ravenhill's house. It was full of paint. Red paint. Red paint that left an ugly stain as it ran down the side of the wall.

Derrick and the guys were out on the sidewalk. Laughing. Cheering. Jeering. Their hands were full of balloons. Their hearts were full of hate. "Come on," Derrick called. "Come on out!"

He leaned back and fired another balloon at the house.

Splat!

This one was blue—and equally as ugly.

Not to be outdone, the rest of the boys started to join in, throwing their balloons as hard as they could.

Splat . . . splat, splat . . . splat.

Red, yellow, blue—balloon after balloon exploded against the house.

The animals on the porch began to panic. They paced back and forth in their cages. They screamed. They howled. They barked crazily.

But there was no movement inside that house.

"What's the matter, old man?" one of the guys yelled. "Afraid of somebody that can fight back?"

There was no movement inside the house because Mr. Ravenhill was frozen in fear. He had flattened himself against the far wall. This was the second attack in two days. He had no idea what was happening—or why. All he knew was that somebody out there meant business. And he knew that if they really wanted to, those somebodies could hurt his animals and destroy his home.

And there was nothing he could do about it.

The buses were one yellow blur as Nicholas raced past them. He was running for all he was worth. Somebody had to stop Derrick. Somebody had to put an end to all of these lies. Nick wasn't sure how he'd do it—but he knew he had to try.

"Come on out, creep! Let's go, chicken!"

Splat, splat . . . splat.

The boys shouted and threw more balloons.

The animals cried and howled in panic.

Finally Derrick had worked up enough courage to break from the boys and head toward the porch. "I'll show that bum. . . ."

For a moment the other kids held back. But as Derrick

flew up the porch steps, they also found their courage and followed. "Yeah, let's get him—let's show that creepy old man!"

Nicholas was still running. He was only a few blocks away, but his throat felt like it was on fire. He was breathing too hard. The autumn air was so cold that it seemed to cut a deep groove into the back of his throat. But he kept running. Derrick was on the porch now. He had ripped off the door to one of the little pigeon cages and was holding the cage high over his head. The birds flew out as quickly as they could. *Crash!* The boy threw the cage down on the porch and laughed as it splintered into a million pieces.

The other kids followed his lead. They pushed over every cage they could find. They ripped open every door that could be opened. Frightened and panicky animals scurried in all directions. And, once the cages were emptied, those cages were smashed into pieces on the porch. One after another after another.

It was a nightmare full of crying animals, broken cages, and laughing boys.

Nick felt it in his legs now—or rather, didn't feel it. His thighs and calves had started to feel like rubber. But he continued to run, pumping as hard as he could.

He turned to cut across the street when he suddenly heard the screech of brakes. He looked up just in time to see a car skid to a stop. It was less than five feet from him.

The driver looked as white as a sheet and started to shout

something. But Nicholas didn't have time for chit-chat. He was off again.

He finally flew around the last corner and saw the old man's house just ahead. But what he saw slowly brought him to a stop.

In front of him was the porch—or what was left of it. Everywhere there were broken and overturned tables, cages shattered and destroyed. And paint—lots of blue, yellow, and red paint—dripping everywhere on the porch, the walls, the steps.

Pleased with their work, Derrick and his friends turned and started to leave. They headed down the steps and didn't even see Nicholas until they were right in front of him. But, as always, Derrick had the right word for the right occasion. "Now who's the hero, kid?"

And, before Nicholas could answer, the boy took off down the street with the rest of his friends. Everyone was laughing and shouting over the victory.

Nicholas watched as they disappeared. Then, slowly, he turned back to the house.

He couldn't believe his eyes. It was awful—like seeing those TV pictures of what a tornado leaves behind. Terrible.

And then Nicholas saw it—or rather, he heard it. Some sort of movement on the porch. Some sort of sound.

Slowly, the boy started toward the porch. He saw more and more damage as he got closer. And then he saw George Ravenhill.

Somehow the man had hobbled onto the porch. But now,

he was on his knees. In his arms he was holding the rabbit. The very same rabbit Nicholas had seen in the cellar. Only it didn't look exactly the same. Now it looked very limp. And, as Ravenhill continued to hold the tiny creature, Nicholas noticed something else. A small trickle of blood was running from its nose across the big man's hand.

Ravenhill heard Nicholas and looked up. For the first time since the cellar their eyes met.

Nicholas gasped.

He didn't gasp because of the sadness on the old man's face. He didn't gasp because of the tear that was slowly moving across the old man's cheek.

Nicholas gasped because of his eyes. They were the same eyes he had drawn the night before. They were the eyes of Christ—the sorrowful eyes—the eyes full of such love and pain.

And, once again, Nicholas heard his dad's haunting words.

"Whatever you do to others, you're doing to Jesus."

NINE

WRAPPING UP

That evening Nicholas and his dad sat in George Ravenhill's living room. The old man listened quietly as the boy explained all that had happened. There were lots of tears and lots of apologies. But, somehow everyone knew that was not enough. A lot of damage had happened because of Nicholas's lie. A lot of suffering. And to think it could all be forgotten with a simple "I'm sorry"—well, that just was not enough.

So . . . the following Saturday, at the crack of dawn, Nicholas was on George Ravenhill's porch scrubbing off paint, fixing cages, and sweeping . . . lots and lots of sweeping.

Nicholas knew that he was forgiven. That was the beauty of being a Christian. If you mess up, no matter how bad,

God will forgive you if you just ask. Plain and simple. That's why Jesus died on the cross—to take the punishment for whatever we do wrong.

Of course, you have to be serious when you ask him to forgive you. Nicholas was serious. So, as far as God was concerned, the boy was perfectly innocent. It was as if he had never sinned. Not a bad deal.

But there was still the mess and there was still the hurt he had caused Mr. Ravenhill.

So, Nicholas was sweeping and sweeping . . . and sweeping.

He was still sweeping when Louis appeared.

"You really didn't see any of that stuff you said, did you?" Louis asked.

"No," Nicholas admitted. "I didn't see a thing."

"Man—" Louis shook his head. "I wouldn't want to be in your shoes Monday. You're going to catch it good."

Nicholas had to nod. It was one thing to be forgiven by God. But quite another to face the other kids. "I should have told the truth" was all he could say.

"Well, it was fun while it lasted" was all Louis could say. Then, after a moment, he got up and walked off.

If anyone knows what fun is, it's me. And the last few days didn't fit into my definition of fun. But, not wanting to dwell on the past, I was determined to make the most of what we'd been through. So as Nick continued to sweep, I sat near one of the animals' watering trays. It belonged to the raccoon—kind of a nice critter if you didn't smell his breath.

"This is real good," I said to Nick, trying to offer encouragement. "I mean us helping like this. Yes, sir. Uh, you missed a spot."

Nick gave me a look.

"What?" I said.

He just shook his head. Finally, after a couple of moments, he spoke. "I really can't make up for what I did, McGee. I mean, I know God's forgiven me and stuff, but . . . I don't know."

Just then Mr. Ravenhill stepped out onto the front porch. In one hand he was holding the rabbit. With all the bandages it looked a little like a mummy, but it did look like it would get better. In the other hand he held a glass of lemonade. It looked good since it was so hot outside.

"When you're through here," he said gruffly, "you can start working on the cellar steps."

"Yes, sir," Nick said.

"Oh, and uh . . . here." Mr. Ravenhill set the lemonade he had been carrying on a nearby barrel. As he hobbled back into the house, he also offered the kid a trace of a smile.

I've got to tell you, lemonade might hit the spot when it comes to thirst. But what really hit the spot for Nick was that smile. It sent a message that we would remember for a long time. Knowing that the man had forgiven us made all the difference in the world.

"You know, McGee," Nick mused, "saying you're sorry is one thing, but to actually do something . . . well, it's like Dad said, it's good for Mr. Ravenhill—and it's good for me."

"You?" I said, slipping into the raccoon's water dish for a little dip. (I figured a few laps around the pool would be good for me.)

"It reminds me . . . ," Nick continued. "It reminds me how much sin—even a little one—really hurts."

Usually I'm not at a loss for words, but this time there was nothing I could add to what he had said. He was absolutely right.

A moment later the raccoon decided to play with me in his pool. Who knows, maybe I reminded him of his rubber ducky. In any case, he wanted to play patty-cake. And since it was his pool, I went along with it.

"Easy boy, that tickles . . . hee, hee," I giggled as the masked animal played with me.

"McGee," Nicholas said, "why don't you do something to help?"

It seemed to me I'd been helping quite a bit these last few days. Anyway, whipping out my scrub brush and shower cap, I figured I'd make the most of my dip in the dish.

"I'd love to, but the Lone Ranger here's offered to help me take a bath."

"Sure," Nick said. "They always wash their food before they eat it."

"Right-o," I said. "They always wash their—" and then it hit me—"FOOD?! NICHOLAS!"

The kid broke out laughing. I couldn't believe it. I was about to become the soup of the day, and Nick just kept grinning like a cat in a room full of mice. And to make matters worse, the crazy raccoon was getting rougher by the minute.

"Nick! You've got to get me out of here!" The animal pushed me hard under the water. I came up coughing and choking.

"Blub . . . bup . . . oooff . . . NICHOLAS?!" And down I went again.

What an awful way to go.

"All right, all right." Nick was laughing. "You're such a scaredy-cat," he said, lifting the raccoon from the bowl.

"Nicholas . . . ," I gasped, clinging to the edge of the bowl.

"Some animals have no taste," he joked as he set the large animal on the ground.

"Very funny, ho-ho, that's real funny," I panted. "You should be in the circus—as a clown, you Bozo!"

He threw me a grin. And, as mad as I was, I couldn't help smiling back. We'd made it through another adventure. A little worse for wear, but a little better off. And it had happened all because of one sin. No wonder God hates sin so much.

Anyway, things were finally getting back to normal. And that was good. But knowing Nick—and knowing me—normal wouldn't stay normal for long. I was sure there was another adventure waiting . . . just around the corner.

McGee and me!

A STAR IN THE BREAKING

BY BILL MYERS AND KEN C. JOHNSON

When he [Jesus] noticed that all who came to the dinner were trying to sit

near the head of the table, he gave them this advice: "If you are invited to

a wedding feast, don't always head for the best seat. For if someone more

respected than you shows up, the host will bring him over to where you

are sitting and say, 'Let this man sit here instead.' And you, embarrassed,

will have to take whatever seat is left at the foot of the table!

"Do this instead—start at the foot; and when your host sees you he will

come and say, 'Friend, we have a better place than this for you!' Thus

you will be honored in front of all the other guests. For everyone who

tries to honor himself shall be humbled; and he who humbles himself

shall be honored."

LUKE 14:7-11, *The Living Bible*

ONE

BEGINNINGS . . .

The creature rose to his feet with nostrils opened wide. The scent of his prey was still fresh. Silently he searched the dwelling for his next victim.

Mostly humans lived there. At times they could be a bother. Today they were of no concern to the creature. Today he sought a vile and smelly beast that had invaded his world once too often. "This loathsome thing must be taught a lesson," the monster reasoned. "And I will be its teacher!"

And a fearful teacher he was. . . .

His large, misshapen head was covered by reddish-orange shafts of hair. On top there were two menacing gray horns. His mouth hung open, and you could see a drooling tongue and sharp, jagged fangs.

But the most hideous feature was his eye—one huge, red, swollen eye in the middle of his forehead. He looked around, back and forth, searching for his victim, who was hiding somewhere among the humans.

Suddenly the eye caught sight of the victim. It was a short distance away, sound asleep! The poor, unsuspecting fool.

But, just to be safe, the monster froze in his tracks. Any sudden movement now might alert the animal. Then quietly, with the speed of a leopard, he moved forward. . . .

Unaware of the deadly stalking game going on in their living room, Nicholas and his two sisters watched TV. But not just any TV—this was *Trash TV*, the kids' game show where the contestants are slimed, gooped, and, you guessed it, "trashed."

Right now one of the kids was having a dickens of a time trying to make it up the "Slime Slide." Each time he tried to crawl up the chocolate-covered slide, his feet slipped out from under him, and down he went in the goop.

Sometimes it was *plop*, sometimes *splat*, or even *slurrrrrrp*. Whatever sounds the kid made, they were no more disgusting than the way he looked. There were worse ways to go, though. After all, drowning in a vat of chocolate probably wasn't so bad. Besides, it sure looked funny. And Nicholas and Jamie sure were splitting a gut over it.

But not Sarah . . .

Sarah was above that sort of thing. Sure, she sat in the room with the other two. Sure, she heard everything that was going on. However, at the mature age of thirteen (almost fourteen) she really was quite beyond all that childishness. Instead, she sat curled up on the sofa, reading one of those Hollywood teen magazines. You know the type, with TV stars all over the cover and antizit advertisements all over the inside.

Little sister, Jamie, on the other hand, was into the show. Normally she's kind of a shy kid. You know, real sensitive-like. In fact, she probably takes everything way too seriously. But boy is she smart. I mean, if you're thinking of coming down with some kind of disease, try to hold off until she gets through medical school because she's the one who's going to find the cure.

Nick was having a good time too. He never missed the show. And he was constantly amazed at how stupid and clumsy the contestants were. He could do better with his eyes closed. In fact, he'd even sent his name in as a contestant. If they'd just pick him, he'd show them. Of course, they'd never pick him. That sort of thing never happened to normal kids. That sort of thing never happened to average, run-of-the-mill people like Nicholas Martin. . . .

The fanged monster moved fast. He was in the kitchen. Quickly he closed in on his sleeping victim. The thrill of the chase raced through him, giving him even greater speed.

Suddenly, one of the humans stepped into his path. It was the older one. The grandma. Probably fixing dinner.

With amazing agility the monster leaped to one side,

narrowly missing a collision. Good thing, too. A collision would have alerted both his victim and the rest of the household.

Catching his breath, the courageous monster focused on his victim. He would have to move quickly now before anything could warn his prey. But "quickly" was his middle name. . . .

Back at the TV, the trashing continued. Only this time the other contestant was the victim. Again there was a lot of squishing and squashing. And again there was a lot of laughing and groaning by the studio audience.

"Oh no," the host yelled. "I hope that doesn't taste as bad as it smells!"

More laughter.

Nicholas and Jamie could only look at each other.

"Yuck," Jamie said.

"Yuck," Nicholas replied.

Sarah, not to be outdone, finally raised her regal head. It only took a moment to judge the situation. Then from her lips came the wisdom only a girl going on fourteen could have. It was a single word. The word she used to describe almost everything in her life these days. She used it to describe all of her friends' actions. She used it to describe the clothes her mother picked out for her. She especially used it when she emptied the cat box.

"Gross," Sarah said. Then she turned the page in her magazine and went back to reading.

Obviously the girl didn't appreciate the finer details of being trashed. She didn't appreciate the oozing orange slime in the hair. She didn't appreciate the maple syrup running from the hands to the elbows and into the armpits. She didn't even appreciate the classical and ever popular pie-in-the-face.

Luckily, Nick did.

Now only a few feet separated the creature from his victim. Opening his gigantic mouth, he stretched his hairy hands high above his terrible head. This approach had been silent and swift. Now, at last, the sleeping beast lay before him—an unsuspecting bag of fur.

The rumblings of a victory howl began low and deep in the monster's throat. It rose and built with unearthly volume until it exploded from his fanged face: "OOOOAAGGHHUBAG-GAGABOOONNESSS!"

(Translation: "I got you now, Fuzz Face!")

Although the monster had won numerous shriek and scream contests (he even had a degree in screech speech), he knew this scream was his best yet.

So did his victim. . . .

The poor animal jumped from his sleep like a flea on a hot rock. In fact, he barely touched the ground as he leaped over my head and raced for protection from my monster mask.

Oh, uh, yeah, maybe I forgot to mention . . . it's just me—McGee. I'm the monster. Or rather, I'm the one wearing the monster fright mask. When I saw that furry freeloader, Whatever, the family pooch (or should I say, "mooch"), run like a rabbit, I nearly fell over laughing.

Now, don't go feeling too sorry for the fuzz ball. He and I

sorta have a running gag going between us. I play gags on him
. . . and he just plain makes me gag! (I think I'm allergic to ugly.)
Anyway, wearing a fright mask was fun. From the laughter going
on in the family room, I could tell the kids were having a good
time too.

I moved in for a closer look. . . .

Back in the living room, *Trash TV* had started to wind down.
The two contestants stood together and tried to grin through
the slime that kept sliding down their faces.

"Nice effort," the host said. He reached out to shake the
winner's hand. As the boy reached out, the host yanked his
hand away. "But keep it to yourself," he snapped.

The host was that kind of guy. His name was Bill Banter.
One minute you thought he liked kids. The next you weren't
so sure. He was funny, though. Always had a wisecrack for
everything. But sometimes you weren't sure whether he was
laughing with the kids or at them. In fact, sometimes you
weren't sure whether he was a great guy or just a smart-aleck
creep.

"Now," Banter continued, "for next week's contestants.
Shena, do we have the cards?"

Some cheerleader-type kid raced up to him with a couple
of cards.

Back in the living room Nicholas leaned forward. He'd
seen this part of the show a billion times. A billion times he'd
hoped they'd read his name, and a billion times they didn't.
Still, he always listened carefully . . . just in case.

"All right . . . from the town of Ashcroft we have Amy Packard." Banter threw the card over his shoulder as if he didn't care. That was part of his image, not caring. "And from Eastfield . . . Nicholas Martin."

For a moment the living room was still. Had Nicholas heard right? Had the man said what he'd said? Even Sarah looked up, a little startled.

Finally Jamie shouted. "That's you!"

Then the room exploded. Everyone started shouting and yelling at once.

"You won, Nicholas! You won!"

"I don't believe it!"

"Way to go!"

"I sent that card in months ago. . . ."

"All right!"

On and on they went, slapping Nick on the back and high fiving. Sarah even managed to lose her place in the magazine.

Bill Banter wasn't done. He was still holding the card with Nick's name on it and talking.

"Shhh, shhh," Nicholas said. "What's he saying? . . . Listen up . . . shhh. . . ."

"Guys," Banter said, looking into the camera.

"Can we get a close-up of this?"

The camera jerked and bounced into a close shot of the card.

"For those of you who think this show ain't art," Banter said, "one of the reasons we chose ol' Nicholas is this little drawing he included."

It was a drawing of McGee. But not just any old drawing: It was McGee as mighty superhero Major Mishap, his chest thrust out, his cape proudly blowing in the wind.

I guess I shouldn't have been too surprised at seeing myself on TV. I mean, fame was bound to be mine sooner or later. It wasn't even one of Nick's better drawings of me. Still, it was me. I have to admit I did look rather dashing in my pose. It's little wonder that the TV audience and Nick and his sisters were all going nuts. How could they resist?

I pulled off the fright mask I was still wearing. After all, Nick and I were on our way to stardom. Wearing a monster mask would only spoil my image as a Hollywood leading man.

In fact, I was sure the harsh light in the living room might already be spoiling my complexion! So I whipped out the sunglasses to protect my baby-blues. Not for me, of course—for my fans.

"All right," the TV host was saying, "that's our show for today. So until next time, this is Bill Banter, saying to each and every one of you Trash Heads . . . hey, make like a fly and buzz off!"

He gave a wheezy little laugh. The music started blaring. The Martin kids kept cheering. Everyone knew things in the house would change. Everyone knew things would never be the same.

They were right. But the changes weren't exactly what any of them thought they would be. . . .

TWO

MUNCHING WITH THE MARTINS

"McGee or not McGee? That is the question."

I delivered my lines with such emotion I held the audience breathless. There I was, high up on the stage, the lights shining down upon my golden mane (you know, my hair). With a flip of my jewel-lined cloak, I pranced about the stage, totally at ease. My flawless performance continued to hold the crowd spellbound.

It was the seventy-fifth annual Shakespeare Fest and Pancake Supper in Griddle Grease, Texas. An artistic delight for theater lovers and syrup slurpers alike.

I, McGee, of course, was its star—the golden boy of stage and screen. It was me they'd come to see! Winners of dozens of awards, *including seven Oscars, six Emmys, five Grammys, four Tonys, and the Lifetime Achievement Award for the most unsuccessful appearances on a TV game show.*

It was me, the matinee heartthrob of millions, who packed the aisles. It was me, an idol among screen idols, who filled this night with greatness. It was the pancakes, pork sausage, poached possum eggs, and peanut butter waffles that filled the audience's bellies. I mean, it was all you can eat for $7.99. Who could blame them for feeding their faces till they dropped?

Unfortunately, that's just what they did. It seemed the audience had all come down with a bad case of stomach cramps. (I'm sure it was the food. It couldn't have been my performance.) In any case, the people were leaving in droves. The massive crowd was cut down to a few thousand . . . uh, a few hundred . . . a few dozen. . . . Okay, okay, there were six left. But I wasn't related to any of them, and they were still awake.

Unfazed by the course of events, I brought the final act to its searing climax. Then fate struck a final blow. I was consumed by my brilliant performance. I was caught off guard by the sudden gasp from the crowd. Was it something I'd said? I looked up. A falling sandbag was about to steal the scene. I made a valiant attempt to escape its blow—to no avail. The sandbag struck me squarely on the noggin (the head, that is). Next thing I knew, I was kissing the stage floor.

When I rose to my feet, I found myself back in reality. The "sandbag" wasn't a sandbag at all. It was a fork! For a moment I tried to pretend it was the instrument of some pancake-packing patron. But I really knew it belonged to my good buddy, Nick.

He had an uncanny way of bringing me out of my daydreams. This was no exception. (Although being clunked on the head with a fork seemed a bit heavy handed.)

While we're talking about reality, I suppose I should admit I wasn't really in a theater. Actually, it was a suppertime at the Martin household, and we were in the kitchen. No stage. No crowd. My faithful audience was just the Martin clan gathering around the table for chow. And they didn't even know I was there.

They weren't exactly eating pancakes and possum eggs, either. It was close, though. Supper was really one of Grandma's homespun specialties: cauliflower and cabbage casserole smothered in onion gravy. With a side order of boiled beets!

Yummy yum! It really set my taste buds to dancing. I'm sure it did Nick's, too. Unfortunately, I was limiting myself to a low-cal diet of Reese's Pieces and root beer floats. I mean, a guy's gotta be light on his feet if he's going to be on Trash TV. Especially if he wants to avoid catching a case of slimeitis. Believe me, this was one contestant who wasn't about to come outta that show looking like a two-legged hot-fudge sundae.

Ah, yes. The show. I was perched on top of Nick's backpack under his chair. I began to dream about the endless possibilities that lay ahead for Nick and me. . . .

This was our big chance for stardom. I pulled out a small hand mirror and brush. Movie contracts, billions of bucks, awards, fame, fast cars . . . and all the quarter-pound burgers you could eat. And maybe, just maybe, a summer home right smack in the center of the freeway! Yeah, that's the ticket!

My mind was abuzz with the dreams only the beautiful people can dream.

Meanwhile, the dinner conversation at the table was buzzing with excitement. The whole Martin family was jabbering about the show. My buddy, Nick, was the center of all the attention.

"What are you going to wear?" Sarah asked as she poked around her plate looking for something resembling food.

"Forget the clothes," I shouted from below. "What's my share of the prize money?"

"Nothing," Nick called down to me. He was sneaking a fork-ful of beets into his napkin.

"Nothing?" Sarah exclaimed.

Just then the phone rang, and Mrs. Mom rose to answer it.

"I don't think they'll let you do that on TV," Grandma offered. (She was right. I know the name of the show is Trash TV, *but I don't think contestants in their birthday suits is the kinda trash they had in mind!)*

"If you win a phone, can I have it?" Sarah asked. Like all teenage girls, Sarah couldn't survive without a smartphone. In fact, if Mom and Dad would let her, she'd probably have one surgically attached to her ear.

"A smartphone?" Mr. Dad questioned. "What about a trip to Hawaii?" (I noticed he pronounced it "How-wa-yah," so I knew what was coming. . . .)

"Hawaii?" the kids exclaimed, mimicking his pronunciation.

"I'm fine," Mr. Dad answered. "How-wa-you?" He raised his eyebrows and did a Groucho Marx impression that would empty any decent theater.

The kids groaned (which sounded a lot like a herd of lovesick camels). One thing about the kids. They know good humor when they hear it. And this definitely wasn't it.

Meanwhile, Mrs. Mom was finishing her conversation on the phone. "Eight-thirty will be fine. See you then." She hung up and came back to the table.

"Who was that?" Mr. Dad asked.

"The counseling center," Mrs. Mom beamed. "They looked at my résumé and want me to come in for an interview." She was obviously pretty pleased.

"Congratulations. That's great," the kids chimed in.

"I'll bet they'll be glad to get someone with your experience," Grandma added.

Mrs. Mom smiled back. Getting a job that would help out in the community was important to her—and counseling was right up her alley. "I hope so," she said.

All this news of Mrs. Mom's possible job had caused the conversation to change tracks. Seemed like everyone forgot about Nick, Trash TV, and all those great prizes we were going to get. Everyone but me, that is.

Once again I began to dream about the glory and fame. Unfortunately I didn't see Whatever, that pesky pooch, round the corner. He was obviously hoping to find some tasty morsel that had dropped from the table. Then he spotted me—and decided he'd settle for . . . a McGee BURGER!

He snapped to attention. Then the killer canine started

toward me. When I saw him coming, I knew I had to think and think fast. No way I wanted to become a feast for Fido!

Bracing myself for battle, I took my first position of defense (which just happens to look an awful lot like running away). I leaped from the backpack and dashed between the pooch's hairy little legs. I raced for the safety of my upstairs fortress (which looks a lot like Nick's drawing table). The mangy mutt turned sharply and was hot on my tail.

Keeping cool, I took my second position of defense: running even faster and screaming for help!

Luckily, I was fast enough to make it up the stairs and up onto the table. Otherwise I would have had to resort to my third position of defense—whimpering and begging for mercy.

THREE

SCHOOL DAZE

Jamie had always looked up to Nicholas. As far as she was concerned, he could do no wrong. Whenever she had questions, she'd come to him for help. Whenever she was in trouble, she knew he'd be there. Most of the time, it was good having an older brother. It gave her kind of a warm, secure feeling. Jamie loved it.

Of course there were other times. . . .

Like when they played "Spies" in the basement. Nicholas always got to be the enemy agent. She always had to be the good guy. One time he had her gagged and tied to some water pipes, just like on TV. Actually, the game was going pretty well. Nicholas pretended to steal some top secret microfilm (which looked a lot like one of Jamie's old beat-up class photos). Then Mom called down that lunch was ready, and the game was over. At least, it was over for Nicholas. In a flash he was up the stairs, plopped down, and gobbling up his tomato soup and grilled cheese sandwich. Mom made great grilled cheese sandwiches.

When she asked where Jamie was, Nick said he guessed she wasn't hungry. That's honestly what he thought. After all, she heard the call for lunch just like he did.

The real reason Jamie wasn't there didn't dawn on him until almost an hour later. Jamie wasn't coming out of the basement because she *couldn't* come out of the basement. Jamie was still tied to the water pipes!

All things considered, though, Jamie still loved her older brother.

Her older brother loved her, too. 'Course, he didn't come right out and say so. In fact, he did a pretty good job of disguising it when "the guys" were around. Still, Jamie always knew that when the chips were down, Nick would be there.

Today was one of those times. Or so she thought. . . .

Jamie and Nicholas entered the school and headed down the hall together—Jamie toward second grade, Nicholas toward fifth. Sarah was the only one who went to a different school. But that was okay. Sarah was the one who was different.

It had been over a year since Sarah had entered that strange and uncharted territory of "teenagerhood." It had been over a year since she'd decided she was too mature and grown up to be seen with the "children." So now it was Jamie and Nicholas, the two "children," who stuck together and helped each other out.

"Mrs. Snyder wants us to draw our favorite animal," Jamie said.

"Yeah, so . . . ?" Nicholas replied.

"So I can't draw a wombat. Will you help me?"

Nicholas threw her a glance. She was smart. There was no doubt about it. Sometimes he forgot how smart.

"What's a wombat?" he asked.

Jamie could only roll her eyes. How could a big brother who was so smart be so ignorant sometimes? Everybody knew a wombat was a . . . well, it was . . . you know, a wombat. And it looked like . . . well, it kinda looked like a wombat, too.

Before Jamie could put all of this into words, they were interrupted.

"Hey, Nicholas, where's your limo?" It was Renee and a couple of her girlfriends.

Great, Jamie thought. As if her brother's mind wasn't mushy enough already. Now it's not that Nicholas was girl crazy or anything like that. It was just that lately it seemed he talked to them more and more. And the more he talked to them, the more brain-dead he became.

"Oh, uh, hi," he said. Not a great comeback and everyone knew it.

Jamie took a deep breath. *Here we go again*, she thought.

"Big stars need big cars," Renee joked. "You're a celebrity now."

For a moment Nicholas wasn't following what Renee meant. Then he remembered: the show! Ah yes, the show. What did she call him? A celebrity? Well now, he really hadn't thought of it that way . . . but it was true. People did watch the show, so they probably did hear his name. Maybe Renee was right. Maybe he was just a little bit of a celebrity. Not a big star, mind you. No, nothing like that. But at least somebody had heard his name . . . and was treating him a little differently.

"All I did is, you know, send in a card," Nicholas said. But Renee wasn't listening. She was already whisking him down the hall, her friends close behind. Nicholas was her pal, and today she wanted everybody to know it.

"This is all so excellent," she said. Then remembering her two other friends, she nodded toward them, "You know Janelle and Olivia."

The girls smiled. Could it be? Yes, the second one, Olivia . . . was she actually blushing a little? Why?

Then it hit him. Maybe it was because of the show! Maybe she heard his name on TV. He glanced at her. She was still smiling . . . and still blushing. Did his fame really have that effect on people? Hmmmm. He didn't know for sure. He did know one thing, though. If it was true, this was going to be one great week.

So down the hall they went. . . .

Renee chattering away.

Olivia blushing.

Nicholas basking in what he hoped was a newfound popularity.

As for Jamie—Jamie, whom Nicholas always looked out for, whom he was so close to, who so desperately needed his help to draw the wombat . . .

She stood in the hallway. Alone. Completely forgotten.

Things were even better for Nick in class. For some reason, Mrs. Harmon was late. While they waited for her to show, more and more kids started to gather around Nick's desk. Along with Renee, Janelle, and (of course) Olivia.

It was great. Nick could do no wrong. Everything he said was clever. Every wisecrack he made brought laughter. I mean, if this was the price of fame, he wouldn't mind paying that bill for a long, long time.

"Con-grat-u-la-tions, Mr. Hollywood." It was Louis. He flashed his biggest grin, his white teeth gleaming out against his dark face, and sauntered up to Nick in his usual "everything's cool" style. The two of them had been good buddies ever since the time Nicholas had gotten trapped in Mr. Ravenhill's house (which everyone had thought was the scariest house in the world . . . but that's another story).

"So, where are the shades?" Louis asked.

"Shades?" Nicholas quipped. "Why would I want to hide a face like this with shades?"

Everyone laughed. He was on a roll, and he knew it.

If there was one thing Louis could do, though, it was talk. "You're right," he said, grinning. "Better get him a paper bag."

More laughter. Maybe a little more than over Nicholas's joke. That was okay. Louis was a friend. Nick could share his popularity with a friend. As long as it didn't get out of hand.

Suddenly the classroom doors flew open. There stood Coach Slayter, as menacing as ever.

"All right, you jokers," he bellowed. "Sit!"

Sit they did. It was as though they were suddenly sucked into their seats.

Power. Coach Slayter loved it.

He stood at the door with a trace of a sneer across his face. It was meant to be a smile. But after twenty years of working with kids, a sneer was the best he could do.

He lumbered toward the desk—his barrel chest and belly swaying as he walked. It all used to be muscle. Back in the good old days—back in the Marine Corps when he terrified the new soldiers at boot camp. When he shouted into their faces and made them quiver like Jell-O. All that was behind him, though. Now, all he had to terrify were the kids at school.

"All right, listen up!"

The kids glanced at one another nervously.

"Mrs. Harmon is sick . . . or somethin'. I'm here as her replacement." He broke into his version of a grin again. "For the *whole* day."

No one groaned. No one dared. At least not on the outside. But on the inside everyone was thinking the same thing: *Why wasn't I lucky enough to come down with the flu? Or the mumps? Or, Why didn't I step in front of our bus this morning?*

Coach carried a soccer ball under his arm. He always carried some sort of ball. He always wore jogging outfits. Well, not really outfits—more like outfit . . . the same one every day. By the end of the week it always had a distinctive odor about it. "Eau de Gym Locker" everyone called it. We'd heard there was no Mrs. Coach on the scene. By the end of the week, everyone could understand why.

"Get out a clean sheet of paper," he barked. "Spelling quiz this morning."

This time a few groans did escape. But that was okay with Coach. At least he knew they were suffering.

As Nicholas reached into his desk for a piece of paper, he caught Olivia glancing over her shoulder at him.

She smiled.

He smiled.

Hmmm, things were getting interesting.

"All right, first word . . . alememanen." He was reading off a sheet of paper. By the way he butchered the word, it was pretty obvious he didn't know what he was reading.

He tried again. "Alemmemmanen."

He tried yet again. "Alemum . . . alemuma . . ."

More laughter.

"Okay, I'll tell you what," he said as he closed the book. "We'll do this a little later. Right now, uh . . ." He was searching the desk for something—anything. Then he spotted it. "Get out your Health Fitness Workbooks and, uh . . ." He madly flipped through the pages. He had to let them know he was in control. "Take a look at page, uh, chapter, uh . . . chapter four."

The kids exchanged glances. It was going to be a strange day. A very strange, long day.

And long it was. But by the time 2:30 rolled around, the coach had finally found something he was an expert at. . . .

"So we had on a draw play up the middle. As soon as I see the linebacker shoot the gap, I spring to the outside!" The coach was so excited he was practically shouting. "Now, you're thinking, *Where's the free safety*, right?"

Of course the kids were doing anything *but* thinking *Where's the free safety?* Some slept. Others stared at the ceiling counting the little holes in the tile. And Nicholas explored the various designs that could be made from wadded up paper and eraser rubbings.

"Well, they're coming on a blitz!" Coach was lost in memories. He could practically hear the crowd cheering. "So I'm heading upfield with a straight shot right for the goal. Suddenly—"

A sharp knock at the door startled everyone—including Coach. Mr. Oliver, the assistant principal, poked his head in the doorway. "Gus?"

Coach Slayter ("Gus" to his friends) was yanked out of his memories and suddenly found himself back in the classroom. No more cheering crowds. No more adoring cheerleaders. No more glory.

"Oh . . . Mr. Oliver," Coach said nervously.

"I didn't mean to interrupt."

"No, uh, please," Coach insisted. He edged closer to the desk, worried about how much Mr. Oliver had heard.

But Mr. Oliver paid no attention to the coach. Instead, he began to search the classroom, looking for someone. "I was just . . . ," he started to say, then he spotted Nicholas. "There you are."

Nicholas froze. What had he done wrong? He was sure he hadn't done anything . . . at least not that he knew of.

"I just wanted to congratulate you, Nicholas," the man said, breaking into a grin, "and let you know how proud we are of you."

Weak with relief, Nick smiled back. He wasn't sure what Mr. Oliver was grinning about, but he figured it wouldn't hurt to grin in return.

"You can be sure that, come this Saturday," Mr. Oliver said, giving him a wink, "we'll all be rooting for you."

Nicholas beamed. Ah, yes, the show. Word had gotten around . . . more than he had dreamed. Even the bigwigs in the office knew. He was a celebrity now—an official celebrity. There was no doubt about it.

The bell rang then. As the kids gathered around Nick's desk, he realized something wonderful: This was just the beginning. He would rise to the top. He would make his school proud, his city proud—maybe even the whole state. He knew that someday soon the name Nicholas Martin would be on everyone's lips.

And actually, it was true. His name *would* be on everyone's lips.

Though not exactly the way he hoped. . . .

FOUR

A NIGHT IN HOLLYWEIRD

Nicholas was a good guy. Everyone who knew him liked him. Maybe it was because he never tried to be too cool. Or maybe because he always treated people the way he wanted to be treated (even if they didn't always deserve it). That was probably it—he treated people like he wanted to be treated.

He wasn't sure where he'd learned that. Probably from his folks. Or from the Bible. Or maybe both. You see, following God was important to Nick. Oh, he didn't make a big deal out of it. It was just that his friendship with Jesus was one of the most important things in his life. He loved God, and God loved him. Plain and simple.

And because of that love, Nick didn't have to go around

trying to be something he wasn't. He didn't have to go around trying to be supercool. (Cool, maybe, but not supercool.) He didn't have to go around putting others down so he looked good. He didn't even have to go around making sure things went his way. Why should he? God loved him. God was his friend. God would take care of him. I mean, what are friends for?

Still, sometimes Nicholas forgot. Sometimes he'd get so carried away with something he forgot God was in charge. He didn't do it on purpose. It just sort of happened. And with all the excitement about the show, and all the attention he was starting to get, well, it looked like this just might be one of those times. . . .

"Nicholas, if you don't turn that light off in ten seconds you'll be grounded for life!" It was Mom calling from the bottom of the stairs. This was only about the zillionth time she'd told him. He had been so busy sketching and daydreaming that he didn't hear her.

He heard her this time, though. It probably had something to do with the "grounded for life" bit.

"All right, all right," he grumbled. With that he tossed the sketch pad onto his night table. He scooted down under the covers and dug out his radio microphone. He whistled quietly into it, and immediately the light over his dresser went out. He whistled again, a lower note this time. The light over his drawing table went out. One last whistle, a higher one, turned off the lamp on his nightstand.

Besides sketching, Nick also liked to invent. It seemed

every week he invented something different. This invention, his famous "Whistle-Activated-Light-Turn-er-Off-er" was one of his favorites.

To be a good inventor, you also had to be a good dreamer—and dreaming was something Nick did best. You name it, and he could dream about it. Being on the show was no exception. What would life be like now that he was almost a star? What would he do with all the money he won? All the fame? All the glory?

He had dreamed about it all through dinner. He had dreamed about it all through his homework. Now he would dream about it all through the night.

Yes-siree, tonight is the night. At last Nick and I are on our way to the famous Grutman's Chinese Theater in beautiful downtown Hollyweird. We're going to have our handprints captured forever in cement. Then we will unveil our new film, Bat Boys Go Ape!

Now, some of you are probably wondering how a world premiere works. Okay, so some of you probably don't care. But for you classier folks who do care, let me tell you how it goes.

A mob of adoring fans lines the street and the entrance to the glamorous theater. Giant spotlights scan the night sky. Among the crowd is the famous film critic Eugene Shallow. He's interviewing the celebrities who have come out to pay tribute to one of their own (that's me . . . oh, and Nick). Listen . . .

"This is Eugene Shallow outside the world-famous Grutman's Chinese Theater. We're awaiting the arrival of the hottest new

star ever to grace the silver screen. Among our fabulous array of celebrities is none other than one of Hollyweird's most explosive actors. In fact, he arrived tonight in a Sherman tank—probably to promote his new movie, Rumbo X: The Next to the Last Final Chapter of the New Beginning!

"Look! He's coming this way! Excuse me, Mr. Rumbo! Mr. Rumbo! What are your thoughts on this grand occasion?"

"Uh . . . wo . . . yoow, hey, oh . . . yooow, uh, Adriaan!"

"Right. Well said, Mr. Rumbo. Hold on folks, here comes yet another international star. That wacky lackey from way down under . . . Alligator Andee. He's arriving in his Kangaroo Caddy. Mr. Andee, what do your folks from the Outback say on a night like this?"

"G'day, mate."

"Very interesting, but it's night."

"G'day, mate."

"Ooookay, fine. You must be memorizing the lines of your next flick."

"G'day, mate."

"All right already."

"G'day, ma—"

"Look, beat it, will you!"

Suddenly the roar of the crowd alerts Eugene to the arrival of the evening's honored guest—me. Oh, right, and Nick, too, if you want to count him.

The front of our limo pulls into view. The band plays the fanfare: ta-da-da-da, ta-ta-da.

The crowd screams hysterically. (And I haven't even told any jokes yet.)

Our extralong limo continues to pull up. Again the band plays for our entrance: ta-da-da-da, ta-ta-da!

The crowd is beside itself (which is okay by me 'cause that means there's twice as many of them!).

Our limo keeps on coming. (We're talking serious stretch here.) Finally the band tries one last fanfare (minus a few trumpet players who passed out on the last blast): ta-ta-da, ta-to tweep!

At last, to the mighty roar of the crowd (and the great relief of the band) our limo finally comes to a halt.

Through the tinted glass window I can see the cameras flash like fireworks. The crowd pushes in for a closer peek at us, their idols.

Now because of my fame, I've grown somewhat accustomed to this kind of attention. Nick, on the other hand, is a bundle of nerves. I guess it's stage fright. So I figure I'd better take the lead and help the kid with his first session of Meet the Press.

It won't be too tough to protect Nick. After all, the press is out basically to see me. They want to get some juicy story for their gossip papers. Or to catch one of my brilliant smiles for the fan magazines. And, of course, my fans are going wild begging for a lock of my hair or clippings from my toenails. (Fans can be weird like that.) But that's the cost of fame.

I adjust my tux and give the kid a look of encouragement. Then we nod to each other and lower our sunglasses into place. (Those flashbulbs can be murder on unprotected eyes.)

It's now or never. I reach for the limo door. I steady myself for the mob of adoring fans that will shower me with praise. I swing the door open and flash the "little people" my best devil-may-care smile—a sure crowd pleaser.

Like a mighty rush of wind comes the crowd's ringing response . . . like a mighty rush of . . . wind . . . comes . . . uh, ahem . . .

The place is as quiet as a library. No, even a library has some lady saying, "Shhhhh!" all the time. This place could pass for a silent movie! What's wrong?

Suddenly it occurs to me: Bless their hearts, they're speechless! Yeah, that's it. They just can't take all of me in. They don't know how to respond to me, here, live and in living color.

Then I hear someone whisper, "Who's that?"

"WHO'S THAT?" What are they talking about? Has Nick gotten out of the limo behind me? I turn around to take a look. No, not yet.

Suddenly I hear a hissing sound. Rats, I told the driver to check the tires before we left. But wait! The hissing isn't coming from the tires. It's coming from the crowd! I don't understand. Don't they recognize me?

I stand a little taller making sure to block their view of Nick. After all, there is no reason for him to experience this terrible mix-up. But when I block him, they hiss even louder.

Finally Nick is able to push his way out. He must be pretty shook up 'cause he starts waving and blowing kisses to everyone . . . as if he thinks they've come to see him! Poor, confused kid.

Then the crowd sees Nick, and the whole place goes nuts! Photographers, security guards, and millions of screaming faces. I don't understand.

I turn to look at Nick. Already a large group of photographers have surrounded him. What a bunch of goofs. I dash over and leap between their cameras and Nick. Otherwise they wouldn't have gotten me in the picture.

From another direction a different group of newspaper reporters cluster around us. This group is dumber than the last. They keep calling out to Nicholas, "Mr. Martin, Mr. Martin, over here. Give us a smile."

How 'bout a brain?! Again I have to leap up in front of Nick to make sure they get me in the shot. There's no telling how many jobs I'm saving tonight. Just imagine what their editors would do if they went back to their papers without pics of me—me, the premier's star.

Each time they try to take a photo of Nick's face, I'm there with mine. I can tell the picture boys are getting on ol' Nick's nerves, too, 'cause every time I have to jump in to save the shot, he frowns.

At last comes the big moment. Eugene Shallow steps to the mike and invites us forward, saying, "Now for the traditional handprints in the sidewalk."

We cross to the concrete and bend down on our hands and knees. I still have to stretch to get into the photos. Boy! Don't these guys realize that they're only getting Nick in the shot? What kind of fan mag can use that?

"Now, gentlemen," Shallow continues. "Will you place your hands in the wet cement? We want this evening to be remembered, just like all the other great moments in Hollyweird history."

This next part you're not gonna believe. . . .

Nick and I place our hands firmly in the cement, and a lone photographer leans forward. Once again I have to stretch to get into the picture (though Nick did provide a nice background).

Then, all of a sudden, Nicholas's hand shoots up behind me. As near as I can tell, he probably sees a lock of my hair out of place and is trying to smooth it. Or maybe he's just overcome with nerves. Or maybe he's put his tie on too tight!

In any case, his hand comes down so hard that my head goes straight down into the wet cement! You can imagine how hard it is to spring back up in time to join Nick in our final picture. Somehow I manage though. A good thing, too, because it's for the cover of Vanity.

Boy, will I look great! (Even with all the cement gunk on my face.) I just know the Hollyweird Hotshots will be calling me tomorrow, begging me to star in their next flick.

Then, somewhere in the back of my mind, I have this feeling . . . This is too good to be true. Somewhere, in the back of my mind, I have this terrible feeling that this bigger-than-life premiere is just another one of Nicholas's bigger-than-life dreams. . . .

FIVE

FANNING THE FAME

The following morning Nicholas was up bright and early. Now that he was a star, he had lots of important decisions to make. What conditioner should he put on his hair? How much of Dad's aftershave should he use (and exactly where should he use it)? And what color sweater would best bring out the sparkle in his eyes?

Then there was breakfast. Gotta watch those empty calories. Gotta keep that waist slim and trim for your fans. Being a public idol isn't as easy as you might think.

Of course the rest of the family went on like nothing had happened. Dad left for work. Jamie was upstairs getting dressed. Sarah was at the kitchen counter madly trying to finish her algebra.

Nick grinned. *You gotta hand it to them*, he thought. *They're doing a pretty good job of pretending everything is normal.* Actually, that was probably best for the family. You know, not to acknowledge that they had a superstar in their very midst. He smiled gently. Too bad they wouldn't be able to ignore his fame forever.

In just one day he had risen from "Nick the Nobody" to, as Mr. Oliver put it, "Nick-I-just-want-you-to-know-how-proud-we-are-of-you." His fame was spreading like wildfire. Who knew what today would bring? Yesterday he'd brought his school's vice principal to his knees. Today, the world.

"Nicholas, you got your bed made?"

It was his mother. What a silly question to ask somebody as important as Nick. But he'd play along. "Sure, Mom."

"Are your clothes picked up?"

"Yes." He was careful to let his voice sound a little irritated. She had to know he wasn't going to play the game forever.

"Mom, you look great." It was Sarah. She still stood at the counter doing her algebra.

Nicholas glanced up from pouring his cereal. It was true, his mom did look good—if you could be bothered with that sort of thing.

"Thanks, honey," she said to Sarah. "Interview day at the center."

He'd almost forgotten. This was her big day. The day to get that job she wanted so badly. But Nick had other things on his mind. More important things.

"Sarah," he asked, "could you get me the milk?"

Without thinking, Sarah reached for the milk on the counter. She brought it over to the table for him.

Nick's response? Not a thank you. Not even a nod of the head. Instead, "What about the sugar?"

A little frustrated, Sarah turned and headed back to the counter for the sugar.

"Okay, guys, I'm off," Mom said as she headed for the door. "Wish me well."

They did, and she disappeared out the door. Meanwhile, Sarah set the sugar on the table.

Nicholas's response? "You forgot my spoon." Sarah glared down at him.

He looked up, waiting. After all, he had too many other things to think about. Being a star was tough business. He didn't have time to wait on himself. Other people would have to start carrying some of that load.

Sarah reached for the sugar.

How kind, he thought. *She's going to sugar my cereal for me. . . .*

Then she threw a handful of it in his face. "I am not your maid!" she sputtered. With that she turned, grabbed her books, and stormed out the door.

Nicholas was stunned. What had gone wrong? Didn't she know who he was? Didn't she know what a privilege it was to wait on him? "Does this mean you're not getting me my spoon?" he asked.

There was no answer. She was already gone.

Nicholas sighed heavily and started to brush the sugar off his sweater. Obviously the poor, dear child was just overcome with jealousy. *That's okay,* he thought with a grin. *She'll get used to it. They'll all get used to it.*

Unfortunately, school wasn't that much different from home. It started okay. Nicholas was just cruising down the hall toward class. Sure, he had his collar turned up like he'd seen on TV. Sure, he had his hair artfully mussed like the college kids. But, hey, looking supercool was part of his image now.

"Oh, Nicholas . . ." Renee appeared beside him.

"Good morning," he said as he continued to saunter on down the hall.

"Listen, do you think you can get me Bill Banter's autograph? The guy's so cool. I mean, he's really funny."

Nicholas stalled. "Well, I . . ."

Since Banter was the host of *Trash TV*, Nick knew he could get the guy's autograph, no problem. But there was something so uncool about one star asking for another star's autograph.

Luckily, Louis showed up before he had to crush Renee's feelings.

"Hey, Nick. Me and some of the guys were thinking we should go down to the studio with you and, you know, check it out."

That idea sounded even better to Renee. "Yeah! That'd be so excellent. We could all—"

Nicholas knew he had to put a stop to this immediately.

He'd heard of this type of thing happening. Once a person became rich and famous, his friends always try to tag along. "I don't know, guys," he said.

Louis and Renee looked at him, surprised.

"What do you mean?" Louis asked.

Nick raised his eyebrows slightly, trying to look super-cool and bored at the same time. "I mean," he said carelessly, "how's it going to make me look? You know, if I come dragging in with a bunch of kids and stuff?"

"Kids?" Louis's never-failing grin started to fail. "So what do you think you are?" Noticing Nick's collar, he reached over and gave it a flick. "Mr. Chuck Berry, with your collar all turned up . . ."

Having no idea that Chuck Berry was a rock and roller, Renee tried to help. "You mean Chuck Norris?"

Louis could only look at her. She could be so dumb sometimes. Before he had a chance to point this out, Nicholas butted in.

"Hey, look, guys. I'm the one who got on the show, all right? Not you. Me. I'll see what I can do. Maybe if you're lucky—"

"Hey," Louis interrupted. "Don't do me any favors."

"Me, neither," Renee joined in.

Nicholas looked at them. There it was again—jealousy. Just like with Sarah. What was wrong with these people? Didn't they know how lucky they were to be in his company? Didn't they know how blessed they were to have his friendship?

By the looks on their faces, it was obvious they didn't. Nicholas gave a long sigh. Too bad. Still, if that was the way they wanted it, that was the way they'd have it.

"Have it your way," he said. With that, he turned and headed down the hall.

The kids could only stare after him. They were amazed. In just a few short days their friend had gone from "Nick the Nice Guy" to "Nick the Knucklehead." All because of one little TV show.

Louis and Renee shook their heads. One little show had filled their friend with so much pride they couldn't stand being around him. If that's what fame did to people, they didn't want anything to do with it—or with Nicholas. . . .

Meanwhile, Mom had been having her own battle with pride. Before the family had moved in with Grandma, before they had moved into the city, Mom had taught at a small junior college. She also worked as a part-time counselor.

So when the counseling center called her about a job, she was excited. Counseling was something she was really good at. When she went in for the job interview, she expected them to offer her something really "juicy." Unfortunately, "juicy" wasn't exactly what they had in mind. . . .

"Mrs. Martin," they said, "we've looked over your résumé. Your training and experience are quite impressive."

She felt the pride start to well up inside. Of course these people were impressed. With all her experience they *should* be impressed.

"Unfortunately, right now," they continued, "we just need someone to answer our phones." Mom couldn't believe her ears.

"We know that's not much of an offer to someone with your experience—but we really need the help. Would you mind considering it? At least for the time being?"

Mom forced a smile. She didn't know what to do. She didn't know what to say. After another moment she quietly stood up. She said she'd think about it. She shook their hands. Then she calmly left their office, got inside her car . . . and exploded!

How dare they! Don't they know who I am? What about all my training . . . my experience?! HOW DARE THEY! Her insides were screaming all the way home.

Later, after dinner, when she had cooled down some, she heard another voice. It was from inside—but this voice was much different. It was asking a different kind of question. . . .

What would God want me to do? Sure, answering phones would be humbling. Sure, it seems beneath me. But they said they really needed someone to help. Maybe God wants me to be that someone.

What? Are you crazy? It was the first voice again—the angry one. *Serving God is one thing. But not as someone who answers phones!*

The second voice kicked in. *But . . . if I've really given him my life, if I really want to serve him . . . does it matter* how *I serve?*

Then . . . *You're better than that! You're better than someone who just answers phones!* As soon as she heard that, she knew

where the first voice was coming from. She knew it was pride
. . . her pride.

Here she was thinking she was so amazing—that she was
better than somebody else, than "someone who *just* answers
phones." As she thought about it, several Bible verses came
to her mind. Verses that reminded her that we're not to think
that way. Verses that reminded her that we are to consider
other people as important as we are.

Mom sighed and sat down. Just for a moment, she'd
forgotten that part of being a Christian means we're to put
other people first. It means we're to treat others like they're
as important—or even more important—than ourselves. It
means looking for ways we can help and serve them.

She knew that when she stopped thinking the Bible's
way—when she started thinking she was better than someone else—well, there's only one word for it: *pride*.

Still, though Mom knew it was pride, and though she
knew it was wrong . . . it didn't go away. It stayed there in
her mind. It kept arguing with her. It kept telling her that
she deserved better.

So there she was . . . knowing what the Bible said, but also
knowing what she felt. What should she do? It was like a war
going on inside her head. Back and forth. Back and forth.
And, at the moment, she wasn't sure which side would win.

That evening, up in his bedroom, Nick was also fighting with
pride. He *didn't* know that was its name . . . not yet. He just
knew that "being better than everyone else" wasn't as much

fun as he thought. He was starting to lose his friends. And he was starting to feel very alone.

It was one thing for Sarah to turn on him at breakfast. That was expected. She was his sister. But to have his friends turn on him, too—that was a little tough for anybody to take. What was wrong with these people, anyway? What was their problem?

Of course, it never dawned on Nick that the problem might be his . . . that he'd let his pride convince him he was better than everyone else.

All he knew was that it was starting to hurt.

Oh well, at least he had McGee. . . .

SIX

ANOTHER FRIEND BITES THE DUST

On the eve of the big show, I was busy with some glamorous activities—I was pressing my pants. Hey, the way I look at it, it's not what you do so much as how you do it. I've got my own style of pants pressing. (But unless you kiddies at home are old enough to order a pizza over the phone without asking permission, leave this chore to your folks.)

First, you make sure you're wearing your best boxer shorts. A guy can look real goofy standing at an ironing board if he's wearing just any old pair of boxers. Me, I like a snazzy design on mine—you know, like little saxophones.

Second, make sure your shirt and tie are buttoned up nice and tidy. That way, if you forget to put on your pants, they'll still let you eat in a fancy restaurant. (As long as you stay seated.)

Now it's time to get down to the actual job of pants pressing. I like to begin with the left leg first. Don't ask me why. I just feel the left side of things gets overlooked a lot. I mean, have you ever noticed people always say things like, "Oh, I'll just take whatever's left." Or, "Um, nobody's home, I guess they left." Then there's the ultimate, "Oh, look . . . nothing's left!"

It hardly seems fair. So I just have a private campaign to keep a left outlook on life. (I know what you're thinking . . . "He's right.")

Anyway, after the left pants leg has been cared for, I usually check the iron to make sure it's not too hot.

I moisten my thumb (uh, you know, I give it a lick), then I lightly touch the iron. If the iron is too hot, my thumb will make a sizzling sound—something like bacon frying in a skillet. If that's the case, I'll drop the iron and scream loud enough to give my tongue a charley horse.

On the other hand, if the iron is an okay temperature, I'll hold it up a second longer and check my reflection (just to make sure my hair is in place).

It was during this ritual that a shadow of doubt crossed my mind. We were going to be on TV, right? The whole world would see me, right? So, although I'm usually a classy dresser, I decided it wouldn't hurt to get a second opinion.

"Hey, Nick. What do you think about these pants with my checkered tie?"

Now Nick is not exactly what you call a "slave to fashion." You know, he doesn't always have to wear the latest styles in the latest colors. On the other hand, I never saw him stick his hair in orange dye or wear floppy red clown shoes. So I expected a fairly decent answer. So much for great expectations.

"Who cares?" he muttered with a shrug, barely looking up from his homework.

"WHO CARES?" I protested. "I'm not going on that TV show in front of all my fans without looking my best!"

"Your fans got nothing to worry about, Mop Top," Nick said, still not looking up. "You're not going on the show; I am."

I immediately saw red. I also saw Nick calmly turning the page of his textbook. What a perfect target . . . so I did the only sensible thing: I let a spit wad fly!

"Oow!" he yelped.

A direct hit. Now for the verbal attack. . . .

"Listen, Sasquatch," I yelled. "You wouldn't be on that show if it wasn't for me . . . you jarhead!"

Nick grabbed a scrap of paper, wadded it into a ball, and let me have it with one of his better comebacks: "Oh . . . oh yeah?" he stammered, as he threw the paper.

Like I always say, Nick's about as clever as a tree stump when it comes to snappy replies. But when it comes to marksmanship (you know, having terrific aim), he's no slouch. The paper wad beaned me right on the noggin.

"Ferret Nose!" he blurted.

Hmmmm . . . Ferret Nose. Not bad. That's raising the stakes.

Whipping up a nearby walnut, I quickly placed it between two pencils and a rubber band and . . . zing!

"Mutant Brain!" I bellowed, but the lucky little stiff deflected my shot with his notebook. This is war!

Meanwhile, downstairs, little Jamie worked on her art project. Try as she might, she just couldn't get the wombat to look like a wombat. It had taken her two hours and ten pieces of paper—but the closest she got was something that looked part warthog and part fox.

The girl definitely needed some help.

She glanced up the stairs. She knew Nicholas was busy. After all, he was a big star now. And besides, the show was tomorrow. He wouldn't have time for little people like her. She bit her lip. Maybe if she went up and asked real politely— maybe he'd give her a hand . . . for old times' sake.

She decided to gather her things and give it a try. She looked up the stairs, took a deep breath, and started forward.

The battle was in full swing. Nick had on his Rams football helmet. He had also scooped up every eraser he could grab from his art table. Now, from his safe position behind the bed, he hurled them at me like cannonballs.

I, on the other hand, never cared for ground battles. I preferred an aerial assault. And I'm not talking Sopwith Camel, either (those are for beagles). This baby was a top-of-the-line, two-tone, baby-blue jobber with a spit-wad flinger mounted on each wing.

I banked left and brought my plane in, her guns ablazin'. . . .
Bop-bop-bop-bop-bop-boingggg!
Got him!

Nick cringed and grabbed a pillow to shield himself. "Take that, Army Dog!" I cried as I brought my bomber around for another attack. We airmen always hurl neat insults like that at our targets. It really shakes them up. Then, just for good measure, we throw in a crazy laugh: "Moo-moo-moo-hooo-hoo-hahahaha!!!!"

Desperately trying to regain his senses, my opponent hurled another Pink Pearl eraser bomb. "You missed me, Pickle Lips!" I heard him scream over the roar of my engines.

It was a lie. I got him fair and square. But for good measure, and to make him eat his words, I swooped down for another attack. . . .

Jamie was at the top of the stairs now—not far from Nick's room. Then she stopped, frowning slightly. What was that she heard? It sounded just like one of those old World War II movies. *That's pretty strange*, she thought. *Nicholas doesn't have a TV in his room.*

Puzzled, she started toward the door.

The smoke from the bomb was so thick it was all I could do to keep from slamming my plane into a wall. The only way I could locate Nick was when he hurled another insult. "You'll never take me alive, Nose Hair!"

What an imagination. I wasn't planning to take the fathead alive!

I took one last look at my bomb payload and checked the ammo rounds. One final pass around the room, dropping everything I had left, would put the whole place up in smoke. If I wasn't going on that show, no one was.

I tossed in another crazed laugh: "Moo-ho-ho-ha-ha-hah!"

Then I dumped my payload. Every corner of the room exploded with bomb bursts and the rocket's red glare.

KA-BOOM!!!

Jamie was right outside Nick's room now. The noise was incredible—she could hear booms, bangs, and rat-a-tat-tats. She paused a moment. Should she open the door?

For the past couple of years things had not exactly been what you'd call "normal." A lot of it started about the time Nicholas first created his cartoon buddy, McGee. Jamie knew that McGee was just a drawing, that he was just a make-believe character Nicholas sketched on his drawing pad. Still . . .

Every once in a while it almost seemed McGee was alive.

Maybe it had something to do with Nicholas always carrying around his pad and drawing McGee in all kinds of adventures.

Or maybe it had something to do with the imaginary conversations Nick pretended to have with his "friend."

Then there were those other times. Times like this one. Times when Jamie could hear all sorts of strange sounds. Sometimes they came from Nick's room. Sometimes they came from the backseat of the car. Sometimes, they came from weird places—like backpacks and cereal boxes!

Sure, Nicholas could just be making those noises himself. After all, he had a pretty good imagination. Still . . .

Jamie had tried a number of times to catch him—McGee, that is—if he was alive. But she'd never been able to. It had always turned out to be just Nicholas and his imagination.

Maybe this time would be different.

She reached out and put her hand on the doorknob. She turned it. Then with a deep breath she threw it open and discovered . . .

Nothing. Oh, there were some erasers on the floor and some wadded up pieces of paper. But nothing else. Not even Nicholas.

"Nicholas?"

Suddenly he popped his head up from behind the bed. He looked kind of funny—all crouched down with the Rams football helmet a little crooked, like he'd just ducked real fast.

"What!?" He was startled.

"What . . ." she glanced nervously about. "What are you doing?"

"Nothing." He also looked kind of embarrassed. He was always embarrassed when people caught him with McGee. Now he figured he'd better make an excuse about why he was on his knees behind the bed. "I, uh, I dropped something. What do you want?"

"I was wondering . . ." She cleared her throat. "I was wondering if you could help me with my wombat drawing."

Nicholas let out a sigh of frustration. Here he was in the middle of World War III, defending the entire free world, and she wanted him to stop and draw a wombat? Come on!

"Jamie, I don't have time for that kind of stuff! Tomorrow's the big show. I gotta get ready."

She glanced around. It didn't exactly look like he was "getting ready." She started to point this out, but he cut her off.

"Besides, what kind of dumb choice is a wombat, any-way?" No sooner had he said the words than he wished he hadn't. The look in his sister's eyes told him clearly that he'd hurt her feelings—badly. He tried to take it back, to make it better. "Listen, uh, if I have time, I'll do it when I get home."

It was too late. He could tell he'd already cut her. Maybe not with a knife—but sometimes his tongue and his words were even sharper than a knife. He hadn't meant to hurt her. It had just happened. It seemed a lot of things had "just hap-pened" lately.

Of course, Jamie tried to be brave and pretend everything was okay. "Sure . . . thanks," she said. But as she turned and left the room, Nick could tell she was pretty close to crying.

He watched as the door quietly shut behind her. He wished he hadn't been such a jerk. But before he could decide what to do . . .

Splat-too-weee!

. . . another spit wad.

"McGee! Just leave me alone!" Nick shouted angrily. Then he looked around. The little critter was nowhere to be found. "You're not going on the show, and that's final!" Nick said, even more angrily. No answer.

"McGee?!"

Still no answer.

"McGee?" This time Nicholas called more softly. He looked around again. Where was McGee? Where'd he go? Finally, he spotted him—he was back on a page in the sketch

pad. His arms were folded. His back was toward Nick. And he was no longer alive. He had returned to just being a drawing.

"All right, fine," Nicholas said. "You want to be that way?" He reached for the sketch pad and slammed it shut. "Be that way!"

With that he tossed the pad across the room onto the floor.

"Who needs a stupid cartoon, anyway?"

Nick was mad. There was no doubt about it. *He* was the star. *He* was the one going on the show. Nobody else. Just *him*. Renee, Louis, Jamie—even McGee—if they couldn't handle it, that was their tough luck.

The room was strangely quiet . . . and Nicholas felt strangely alone. He threw one last glance to the sketch pad.

It lay on the floor, silent and still.

Forget him. Forget them all. He didn't need them! He didn't need any of them! Not even McGee!

Nicholas lay down on his bed, his head swimming with anger, with hurt . . . and with pride.

Now he was alone. Completely alone.

Well, that was okay. Because tomorrow was the show. And he'd show them. He'd show them all.

SEVEN

FINAL GOOD-BYES

The clock clicked to 7:00 a.m., and the alarm went off.

This was no ordinary alarm. It wasn't one of your blaring buzzers—the type that barges into your sleep screaming, "I don't care how good this dream is, it's time to get up!" Nor was it one of those useless radio alarms. You know, the type you can sleep through if you really want to.

No, this was a one-of-a-kind, Nicholas Martin custom-designed alarm. So, of course, it was different.

For starters there was the clown with the pinwheel. As soon as the radio clicked on, the pinwheel started to spin. It lifted ol' Bozo off the clock and into the air until he crashed into a black, supersonic spy plane . . . which shot across the room on a line until it hit the target on the opposite wall

. . . which triggered a red boxing glove

. . . which dropped and banged into a homemade sign that began flashing ALERT! ALERT! ALERT!

. . . which gave off the appropriate alarm sounds

. . . which made sure Nick would wake up.

Simple, right?

Only this time it didn't work. Mainly because Nick was already awake.

He'd been up for hours trying on one shirt after another. Then, when he finally found the right shirt, his pants were wrong. So he began the same thing all over again with his pants. Now at last he'd found the right combination. (He had to—he was running out of clothes.)

He stood in front of the mirror and put the finishing touches on his tie. Ah, yes, the tie—something he only wore to weddings (and the one funeral he'd been to). It's not that he hated ties. It's just that, well, he had this thing about breathing. He liked to do it. And ties, he figured, had this thing about not wanting him to do it.

He gave the tie one final pull to make it nice and tight. Nice and uncomfortable, too. But, hey, he had an image to keep up.

Finally his eyes wandered to a sketch of McGee he had tacked on the wall. He was in his Major Mishap costume—complete with flying cape and fearless grin.

Nicholas felt his heart sink. He and Major Mishap had

been through so much. They had solved some of the toughest crimes together. They had arrested some of the baddest of bad guys. Now there was no life to the major. Now, he was just a drawing on a piece of paper stuck to the wall.

Nick tried to look away. He did, but only for a second. Soon his eyes were back to the drawing. He could feel the start of something hard and aching in the back of his throat. The two of them had had so much fun together. Now . . .

He looked over his shoulder to the sketch pad. It was still lying on the floor, where he had thrown it. It was still closed. And silent.

The lump in Nick's throat was growing. He tried to swallow it, but it stayed. He and McGee were best friends. Or, at least, they had been. Now . . .

Nick tried his best not to think about it. But he knew he was going to miss McGee. He was going to miss him a lot.

He turned back to the mirror and checked himself out one last time. Satisfied, he crossed to the door. It felt strange not to have that sketch pad under his arm. He'd never been anywhere without it. Still, he wasn't going to beg McGee to come—no way.

Nick grabbed his coat and stopped at the door. He wanted to look back one last time. He wanted to see McGee standing there. He wanted to say, "Hey, McGee, ol' pal, I'm sorry. Come on, Bud, you're just as important to me as any old TV show. Let's go, let's do it together like we always do."

But Nicholas wouldn't.

He couldn't.

After all, he had his pride.

Finally, he stepped out into the hall and closed the door behind him.

The pad lay on the floor—lifeless and unmoving.

EIGHT

A FALLING STAR

The first thing Nicholas noticed was how drab and ordinary everything looked. After all, this was a TV studio! This was the home of Bill Banter and *Trash TV*! But as Nick and his family pulled into the parking lot, he thought the station looked just as dull and boring as any other building. No glitter, no spotlights, no names in lights. Just a dirty brick building with a few satellite dishes stuck on top.

That was the outside. The inside held even more disappointments. Like the building, the receptionist looked bored, tired, and seemingly lifeless. Nick couldn't understand. Didn't she know what an honor it was to be working there? Didn't she know how excited she should be? After all, she was rubbing shoulders with the stars!

He wanted to ask her about it, but he didn't have time. As soon as his dad told the woman who they were, she rose from her desk, telling them to follow her. She led them down a narrow, dimly lit hallway. Nick looked around. There, right there on the walls, so close that he could reach up and touch them, were photos of all sorts of grinning celebrities. Bob the weatherman, Julie Shimaskaki the news anchorwoman, Sandy from Afternoon at the Movies. They were all there! Nick could feel his heart begin to pound. This was it. This was *really* it.

With a grunt the receptionist pushed at the heavy door of the soundstage. There was a quiet woosh as it opened. They were hit with a wave of cold air from the air-conditioning. That's not all they were hit with. They were also hit with color. Lots and lots of color. And light.

Nick sucked in his breath. Here they were. Right on the set of *Trash TV!* There were the Slime Slides to the left—*the* Slime Slides—the very ones he had seen so many times on TV! And over there, oh, over there was the scoreboard. There were the bleachers, where the audience would boo and hiss and cheer and clap. Nick couldn't believe his eyes. He was really here.

"I don't give a rip about your budget! My contract calls for a hairdresser, and a hairdresser is what I expect!" The voice was shrill and loud and demanding. It was also strangely familiar. Nick squinted into the bright lights to see who it was.

"Bill, she's got the flu. Let somebody else take care of your hair, at least for today—"

"Shut up and get me that hairdresser! Do you hear me? I want that hairdresser, and I want her now!"

It was Bill Banter! He stood not more than ten feet away! But this wasn't the Bill Banter Nick had seen on TV. This wasn't the good-looking, always-got-a-smile, wisecracking star everyone knew and loved. This guy was scrawny, skinny, and screaming.

"Bill—"

"Now!"

"Bill—"

"NOW!!"

"All right, all right. . . ." The other man moved off, looking like a whipped puppy. Banter went back to studying his clipboard. Then he felt Nick's eyes on him and looked up.

Uh-oh, Nick thought. *I'm in for it now.*

But instead of screaming or throwing another temper tantrum, Banter suddenly broke into a grin. Not just any grin. This one was so big you could see every one of his perfect, pearly whites.

Nicholas returned it nervously. He was a little confused. How could someone be such a creep one minute and such a nice guy the next? He didn't have long to think about it, though. Suddenly Banter crossed over to him and stuck out his hand for a shake. Nick took it. It was soft and cold and wet. "You must be Nicholas Martin. Glad to meet you."

"Hi," was about all Nick could say. Even that sounded

more like a squeak than a word. It's not that he was a little nervous or anything like that. He was a lot nervous. This was Bill Banter. *Bill Banter, for crying out loud!*

Before Nick could say anything else—like tell Banter how excited he was or how funny and cool all his friends thought Banter was—the host turned and started shouting again. The smile on his face had disappeared as quickly as it had appeared. It was like he had some sort of "nice person" switch that could be turned off and on. Apparently he'd just found the off position again.

"WHERE'S THAT HAIRDRESSER? SYDNEY, YOU'VE GOT EXACTLY TEN SECONDS TO GET ME THAT HAIRDRESSER!"

"Places everybody; we're on in five," a pleasant-looking man with headphones called out to the crew. Everyone began to run and make last-minute preparations.

Nick was up in the makeup chair. A lady was putting the final touches to his face. It was kind of embarrassing for a boy to get tan goop smeared all over his face. It was even more embarrassing smelling like your sister's makeup drawer. Still, if this was what a star had to put up with, then Nicholas knew he'd better get used to it.

He threw a glance over to the chair beside him. It was his opponent. The person he would be competing against on the show. Poor thing. It was pretty obvious she didn't stand a chance. Not against him.

For starters she was a *she*. Nick smiled smugly. Everyone

knows boys are better at this sort of stuff than girls. Second, she was about as skinny and weak looking as they came. Now it's true, Nick wasn't the world's greatest jock. It was just that he was sure he'd have no problem beating this pathetic little creature. In fact, he could probably beat her with one arm tied behind his back—or maybe two. Or maybe both arms and one foot. Or maybe . . . well, even if they tied whatever else could be tied back there, he knew he could still beat her.

In short, it was going to be a massacre.

Nick didn't mean to, but he couldn't help smiling. Today was going to be better than he'd even thought.

"Hello, again, and welcome to *Trash TV*!"

The music blasted away. The kids in the audience clapped and cheered.

Nick tried to swallow, but his mouth was as dry as cotton. He stood backstage behind the set, waiting to go on. For a minute he thought about praying. Then he pushed the thought out of his head. He didn't need to pray. He'd made it this far on his own without bothering God. Why should he start now? Besides, he'd seen the girl he was competing against. Beating her would be a piece of cake.

He heard Bill Banter carrying on, being his usual witty self. But from backstage, the man sounded hollow, kind of empty. Maybe it was because Nick had seen what he was really like—when he was screaming for a hairdresser. Or maybe it was because he had seen him without the makeup, the fancy clothes, and the adoring fans laughing at his every word.

As Nick waited, he reached out to touch the back of the set. It was the same brightly colored set he had seen so many times on TV. But when he touched it, a piece broke off in his hand. He was startled. When he'd watched the show from home, everything had looked so sparkling, shiny, and expensive. Close up he saw it was only Styrofoam. Cheap, flimsy Styrofoam. As for the sparkle and shine, it was just spray paint and regular ol' glitter—the type you could buy at any hardware store.

Apparently, just like Bill Banter, nothing was as it appeared. Not when you got up close.

Banter was in his best form. "Our victims, er, contestants this week are . . . Amy Packer, from Ashcroft! Come on out, Amy!"

The kids cheered and clapped as Amy raced to her place beside Banter.

"And Nicholas Martin, from Eastfield!"

This was it! Nick took one last breath and ran out into the lights.

There was Banter grinning as big as ever. There were the cameras sending his picture across the universe. And there were the kids in the audience—all clapping and cheering for him. *Him,* Nicholas Martin, up-and-coming superstar.

"Okay, my precious piggies," Banter teased, "you know the object of the game. Trash your opponent as often as possible, and add up those points. The one with the highest score at the end of the game becomes our grand prize winner! So let's play . . . *Trash TV!*"

Before Nick knew it, an assistant swooped down and shoved a cowboy hat on his head. Then she tied a holster around his waist. Instead of guns, though, it held squeeze bottles—one full of ketchup, the other full of mustard. Next, she shoved Nick to the center of the stage to face his opponent.

"Okay, we're in the Western mode here." Banter pointed to Nick. "You're Wyatt Burp." Then he pointed to Amy. "You're Annie Oafly. You've got fifteen seconds to see who's the greatest food fighter in the West. Turn your backs to each other, and at the count of three, draw."

Nicholas turned. This was going to be easier than he thought.

"One . . . two . . . three . . . DRAW!"

Nick spun around and began to squeeze the bottle. A direct hit! He got wimpy little Amy, and he got her good!

"All right, trash her, TRASH HER!!" Banter rooted him on.

Nicholas went in for the kill. First the ketchup, then the mustard. Then the ketchup again. He was practically drowning the little girl. He completely covered her hair and face with the slimy goo.

Finally the buzzer went off, and Nicholas raised his hands in victory. The audience went crazy—clapping and cheering and hooting. Nicholas had never felt such excitement in his life. He had never experienced such glory. Fortune and fame were his now! He could smell it. He could taste it. They were all his for the taking!

"All right!" Banter shouted over the cheers.

"Nicholas wins that round with a big ten points!"

Nick kept on beaming, basking in the glory. He didn't bother to look over at Amy. She was history.

Had he bothered to look, he might not have been so sure of himself. Because he would have seen someone seething in anger. He would have seen someone setting her jaw, getting ready for revenge.

Now Nick and Amy stood behind two counters. A dozen pies were in front of each of them as Banter introduced the next competition.

"Now this ain't no piece of cake. In fact, it's Pie in the Eye." The audience snickered. "Are you ready?"

The kids nodded.

"One . . . two . . ."

Nicholas was much more relaxed now. In fact, he even took a moment to look around. There was his family off to one side, grinning away. Well, why shouldn't they be? He was doing them proud. Then there were the kids cheering him on. Why not? He was giving them a great show. Finally, there were those cameras—where Louis and Renee and Coach Slayter and Mr. Oliver and McGee and the whole world were watching . . . sharing in his victory.

". . . three, THROW!"

For a second Nicholas hadn't heard Banter. The boy was so lost in his glory that he wasn't ready.

Amy, on the other hand, was.

She landed a banana cream pie smack dab in Nick's face. Before he could wipe his eyes to see what was going on, she got him again . . . and again. One pie after another came flying in.

Nicholas began to cough and sputter. He liked banana cream, but not this much. If he could just get his goggles cleaned off . . . if he could just see where his pies were so he could grab them. Better yet, if he could just see where Amy was so he could dodge her pies. But he couldn't— and the pies just kept on coming.

At last the buzzer went off, and it was over. But not really. Not by a long shot. The attack continued. . . .

Amy kept right on throwing—one pie after another after another. She was incredible. It was like she took out all her anger from the last event and put it into throwing the pies. She wouldn't stop! She just kept right on throwing. Nicholas kept right on coughing and sputtering. It got to be so bad that Banter finally had to move in and start pulling her away.

"All right, all right," he laughed. "We have a real live one here, folks!"

At last Nicholas had a chance to wipe off the whipped cream and see what was going on. Then, when he saw what he saw, well . . . he wished he hadn't seen it. The audience was going crazy. They were clapping and laughing and shouting. Unfortunately, they weren't clapping and laughing and shouting for him. Not anymore. Somehow they had started to side with Amy.

Weird, Nicholas thought. *You lose one little event and suddenly everyone turns on you.*

"That's okay," he muttered. "I'll show you. I'll show you all."

The next event was no better than the last.

It was a beanbag toss. Something anybody could do, right? After all, you just throw a beanbag through a hole in the wall. The only problem was that the wall was halfway across the studio. Oh, and there was one minor flaw . . . Amy was the star pitcher on her Little League team.

"All right! Amy gets another one! And another one! And another one! Come on, Nicholas, you're getting slammed!" (Banter never showed much sympathy for losers.)

As for the crowd—they were going nuts. They cheered and laughed and hissed. Only this time twice as loud. They were having the time of their lives watching this little twig, this little wimp of a girl massacring Nicholas. *Nicholas!* The Great Nicholas Martin.

Finally the buzzer sounded, and the humiliation was over. Well, not quite. The loser had a little reward coming. Suddenly, from high above, a huge bucket of flour dumped all over his head.

If the audience was having a good time before . . . well, they were rolling in the aisles now.

Once again Nick was coughing and choking—and covered with food. Only this time, instead of banana cream, he looked like a giant powdered doughnut. A very embarrassed and humiliated powdered doughnut.

Things were getting bad for Nicholas—very bad. What had once been a dream too good to be true was quickly turning into a nightmare. Still, it wasn't over yet. . . .

Now they were at the Slime Slides. Yes, *the* Slime Slides. Each slide was coated with thick, oozing chocolate. The idea was to climb up your slide, grab the flag at the top and slide back down. Simple. Except that you also had to balance a raw egg on a spoon, which you held between your teeth. Oh, and if you slipped, there just happened to be a giant vat of chocolate waiting for you at the bottom.

Nick wasn't worried. He'd seen it done a zillion times. He could go up this slide in his sleep.

He crouched down at the bottom of the slide, waiting for the starting pistol. His muscles were tense, ready to leap into action. He'd had a couple of bad breaks before. That was all. He could make up for it now.

He stared at the flag . . . waiting.

Slowly, Banter raised the starting pistol.

The kids continued to cheer and jeer.

Nicholas paid no attention. He would win this one. True, he was behind in points. But if he put all his concentration into winning the Slime Slide, he could regain his lead, his dignity—and his pride.

He continued to stare . . . waiting . . . thinking . . . barely breathing.

Slowly Banter started to squeeze the trigger.

Nicholas continued to concentrate on the flag—his muscles taut, ready to thrust him into victory.

Finally the gun fired.

And they were off!

Well, at least Amy was. Nicholas had concentrated so hard on the flag that he hadn't watched his feet. As he shoved off, his right foot slipped out from under him. He fell face first into the thick gooey chocolate.

That was only the beginning.

Before he could catch himself, he landed belly first on the slide . . . and he started to slip. He tried to grab the sides, but they were too slippery. It was only a couple of feet, but he couldn't stop. It was like a slow-motion nightmare. Then suddenly there was no slide under him. After a moment there was a tremendous thwack! as Nicholas did a perfect belly flop into the vat of chocolate. The sound echoed around the room as he slowly sank into the goop.

The audience screamed and roared with laughter.

"Oh no," Banter howled. "He's done it again!"

Nicholas wasn't giving up. He scampered back to his feet. Unfortunately he had no idea how slippery chocolate could be. Immediately his feet slid out from under him, and *splat!* He landed back in the chocolate . . . rear first.

By now the cameramen and crew were also laughing.

Again he tried, and again his feet slipped out from under him. And again.

The audience howled so loud they sounded like a pack of wolves.

Finally Nicholas struggled back to his feet. By now he looked very much like a chocolate-covered peanut. He was totally covered with brown goop. In fact, if it hadn't been for the whites of his eyes you wouldn't have even known which direction he was facing.

It didn't matter. Amy had made it to the top.

She grabbed the flag and gracefully skated down the slide. There wasn't a spot of chocolate on her as she waved the flag at the cheering audience.

They began to chant, "A-MY! A-MY! A-MY!" It was worse than Nick could have ever imagined.

And so it went. Event after event after event. Fortunately, when he thought about it later, Nicholas couldn't remember everything. Only bits and pieces. Like the strawberry syrup poured over his hair. Or the pepper pile he fell into. (You'll never appreciate sneezing until you've fallen into a three-foot pepper pile.) Or the pillow fight.

Ah yes, the pillow fight. After the third or fourth hit, Amy's pillow exploded. Chicken feathers flew everywhere. Mostly they flew on Nick, who was still drenched in sticky chocolate. So wherever a feather landed, it stuck. Which meant they stuck everywhere!

In just a few minutes Nick had gone from Conquering Hero to Pie Face, to Powdered Doughnut, to Chocolate-Covered Peanut, to something the folks at Kentucky Fried Chicken might be eyeing. It was terrible.

All this *plus* the constant laughing, mocking, and finger pointing from his once-adoring audience.

Also, let's not forget those cameras. Those wonderful, friendly cameras that were catching the entire fiasco for the whole world to see. (When the cameramen weren't giggling and bouncing them in laughter, that is.)

Basically, Nick wanted to disappear. He wanted to crawl into a hole and hide. But search as he might, there were no holes available.

How could this have happened? He had been so sure of himself. He *knew* he was better than this little girl. He knew he was better than just about anyone . . . his sisters, his friends, even McGee. After all *he* was the one who got on the show. *He* was the star. *He* was the one who was going to clean up on his helpless little opponent. So what in the world had happened?

Finally the last buzzer buzzed, and Nick was hustled off the set. Past the sarcastic Banter. Past the snickering cameramen. Past the shrieking audience.

At last he was out of the glaring lights of stardom. But it was all there. It was all there in his memory. The pain, the embarrassment, the humiliation. What had gone wrong?

It wasn't until the ride home that the answer started to come. Everyone was pretty quiet in the car. They didn't know what to say. That was okay. Nick probably wouldn't have heard them anyway. He just sat in the backseat, silent and aching, trying to hold back the tears.

Then, slowly, something started to come to his mind. Of all things, it was a Bible verse. A *Bible verse?* He didn't need a Bible verse. Not now. But it came to his mind, and there was nothing he could do about it. It was a verse he had to memorize for Sunday school months ago. It didn't make a lot of sense to him then, so he never gave it much attention. It was just one of those verses you learn without ever knowing what it means. But for some reason it came back to him.

And for some reason it finally started to make sense. Not all at once, mind you. But by the time they finally got home, he began to understand:

"Everyone who tries to honor himself shall be humbled; and he who humbles himself shall be honored."

NINE

REUNION

I'd seen the whole thing on the TV. At first I was kinda grinning when the little goof got clobbered. Then it got worse and worse. Then, when you were sure it couldn't get any worse, it got worse some more.

Poor kid.

I mean, anyone who's ever waited too long to throw a firecracker once it's lit knows that making a mistake can be a painful thing. But making a mistake in front of the whole world can almost finish you for good.

I guess that's how Nick must have felt. He must have figured everything was ruined. No fans. No fame. And, what's worse, no friends.

That's where he was wrong.

These last few days it seemed like our whole world had turned upside down. Sometimes that kind of thing shakes you loose from the people you care most about. If you stop to think about it, though, you'd find that nothing's more important than those people—'cause they're the ones who never stop caring and believing in you.

After seeing him get slaughtered on TV, I knew Nick needed to know that. I also knew I needed to tell him. Finally I heard the car drive up, and I heard him clumping up the stairs to his room. At last he threw open the door. The kid looked beat. I mean, he gave a whole new definition to the word whipped.

He didn't see me, and he didn't say a word. He just dragged himself over to the bed and collapsed. Poor guy.

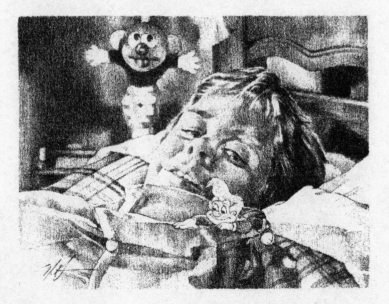

I quietly crossed to the bed and climbed up onto the pillow. Nick's eyes were clenched tight. Even at that a tear managed to sneak out and slowly move across his cheek. I eased down on the pillow beside him and gently leaned against his shoulder.

After a minute he opened his eyes.

I gave him my best "You okay, Little Buddy?" look. Then I reached out and gently patted him on the shoulder. And he did what any best buddy in the whole wide world would do—he smiled.

We were gonna make it. We were gonna regroup, learn from our mistake, and probably take more lumps along the way.

But we were gonna do it together.

TEN

WRAPPING UP

Monday was lousy.

The week before, Nicholas had hoped everyone would watch the show. Unfortunately his wish had come true. Now it seemed like everyone had something to say.

"Nice work, champ . . . or should I say 'chump'?"

"You stunk so bad I could smell it over my TV."

"Look out! It's the human Hershey bar!"

Of course he pretended to laugh and smile along with them. Inside, though, whatever was left of his pride just kept on dying.

Even Olivia treated him differently. Oh, she still threw him an occasional glance from time to time. But the way her eyes crinkled and the way she covered her mouth as she leaned over to talk to her friends . . . well, it was pretty obvious she was laughing. She wasn't laughing with Nicholas, though. She was laughing at him.

Finally the three o'clock bell rang. At last Nicholas could head for home. He moved out the front doors and down the steps. It was raining. Somehow that didn't surprise him.

"Hey, Mr. Big Shot! What happened?" It was Louis. Well, at least here was somebody who would understand—someone who would still be his buddy.

"So, where are all your friends now?" he said, smirking. Before Nicholas could answer, Louis turned and headed off, snickering all the way.

Nick took a deep breath and let it out. He couldn't blame Louis. He knew he'd been a jerk. In fact, he'd been a certifiable, cream-of-the-crop creep. Whatever his friends dished out over the next few days he probably deserved. He knew it wouldn't last forever—but he also knew it wasn't going to be a lot of fun.

"Not a great day, huh?" It was Jamie.

Nick couldn't help but grin. It was nice to finally see a friendly face.

"Sure you want to hang out with the all-school idiot?" he asked.

"That's okay, I'm used to it."

He wasn't sure if that was a compliment or not. Still, he knew she meant well. Even though everyone else had turned their backs on him, Jamie was still there. His little sister. True to the end.

"So tell me," Nicholas asked, "how's that wombat of yours coming?"

Jamie grimaced. "It's due tomorrow. Jenny Michelson says it looks like a porcupine from Mars."

Nicholas tried to swallow back his laughter. "Well, maybe I can give you a hand with it."

"Hey, guys . . ."

They looked up. It was Mom. She was standing, waiting in the rain.

"Mom, what are you doing here?" Nicholas asked in surprise.

"I've been answering phones at the counseling center."

They joined her and headed for the car.

"You mean you took the job?" Nicholas asked. With the show and all he'd almost forgotten about the decision Mom had had to make about the counseling center job.

"Yep," she said as she smiled at Nicholas. "I'm afraid you're not the only one getting to learn humility."

Nicholas grinned. "So that's what I've been learning."

She reached over and put her arm around him. "That's what we've both been learning, kiddo."

"Not a lot of fun, is it?" Nicholas teased.

Mom grinned back knowingly. "It's something we all need," she said with a sigh.

They arrived at the car, and she opened the door for them to climb in. "God gives strength to the humble," she quoted. "But flattens the hotshots."

Nicholas had to laugh as he crawled into the car.

"*Truer words were never spoken,*" *I said to myself as Nicholas and I settled into the backseat. However, it seemed to me that they could be spoken a bit more poetically. So I lifted up the cover to my scratch pad and added, "Sure, it's like I always say, 'If you think you're a hotshot, watch out for game shows with chock-o-lot!'"*

"McGee," Nick groaned. The kid never did have a great sense of humor. Then he shot me a sly smile. "How 'bout: 'If you keep making jokes so bad, watch out for slamming sketch pads!'"

Boy, his rhymes were worse than mine.

"Uh, no . . . ," I gently corrected. "Oh, here we go: 'If you're a kid that's stuck-up, plan to get mustarded and ketch-upped.'"

The last thing I saw was the curl of Nicholas's lip just before he brought the sketch pad cover down on top of me! I made a last-ditch effort to reason with him. "Hey, wait a min—"

Slam! went the pad.

If you've ever tried talking with your jaws wired shut or with a mouth full of biscuits, you can understand why I suddenly sounded like this:

"Mikomus! . . . Met me out of mere . . . MIKOMUS!"

The worst part about trying to talk with your mouth closed is that you can still hear what other people say.

"Did you say something?" Mrs. Mom asked as she climbed into the other side of the car.

"It's nothing, Mom," Nick replied.

Nothing! Why that little sneak! "MIKOMUS! OPEN MISS MAD!" I shouted. It was no use. His bony little hand just held the cover down more firmly.

"Nothing at all," he chuckled, and I could tell he was smiling.

Okay, kid. You just keep it up, *I thought*. Enjoy yourself while you can. I already know about the next chapter in our little adventure. And believe me, buddy boy, it makes this last episode look like a picnic . . . with ants . . . (and maybe even a few uncles)!

McGEE and me!

THE NOT-SO-GREAT ESCAPE

BY BILL MYERS AND KEN C. JOHNSON

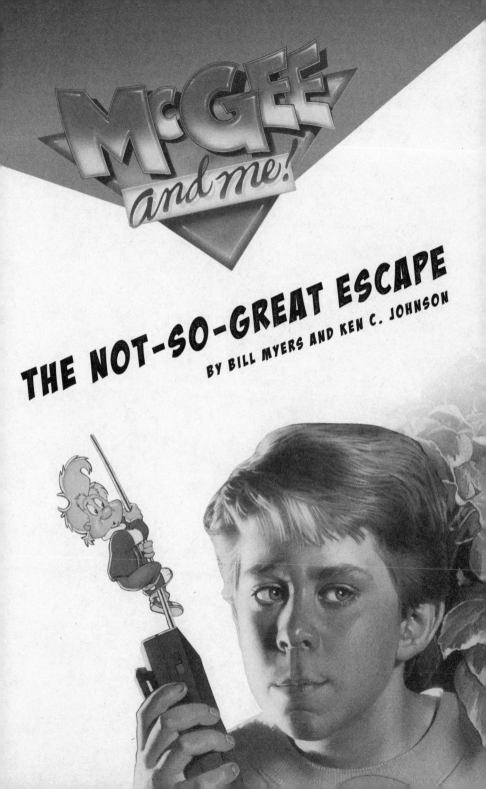

Fix your thoughts on what is true and good and right. Think about things

that are pure and lovely, and dwell on the fine, good things in others.

PHILIPPIANS 4:8, *The Living Bible*

ONE

THE SPACE CREEPER
STRIKES AGAIN

Thirty-two right, fourteen left, seventeen right, and finally noth-ing left . . . to do but wait, that is. Then slowly the lock on the door of my lunar prison cell began to open. I stood there, gripped with suspense. The hefty door swung wide, revealing what I'd worked on for these many months—my freedom. Though it had taken only a few moments and some brain-bending calculations to program the lunar lock and figure out its combination, it had seemed like days. Okay, so it had been days: 136 days to be exact. But, hey, who's counting? I never really was that good in math anyway.

I was counting on one thing, though: getting out of there! There had never been a prison in the star system that could hold the sinister Space Villain for long. Besides, I needed a change of scenery. Between choking down the galactic glob they called food and playing several games of "stare down" with the four walls, this hadn't exactly been a summer vacation. So, with a song in my heart and a sneer on my lips, off I went.

I snaked my way swiftly and quietly down corridor after darkened corridor. A thousand thoughts raced through my head: Had I tripped the alarm? Were the android guards on to me yet? Was my hidden space pod still intact and waiting for me in Quadrant Three? Is Colonel Crater's Fried Chicken open this time of night?

Suddenly a phaser blast pierced the darkness. It ricocheted right in front of my feet. As I frantically dodged the blast, I realized one of my questions had been answered: The guards were definitely on to me.

I moved down the corridor, slipping through one hallway and down another with moves that would have made Justin Bieber turn green with nausea . . . uh, envy. The android guards were hot on my trail—this little game of blast attack was getting old fast. If I could just think of something to throw them off track. Maybe get the goons to sit down and swap nuts-and-bolts recipes or something. Unfortunately, I had left my Betty Cosmos Cookbook back in my cell. So instead I chose to stick to my original brilliant plan: Run!

Another series of laser bursts grazed past my heels and exploded in front of me. The shots tore a hole in the air vent beside me. Aha! *I thought.* Their brainless blasting has created an escape route. *Amidst a blaze of laser fire, I dove for the air duct and squeezed inside. It was just big enough for a notorious space villain of my size.*

As I scooted down the shaft, I let out a hideous cry to taunt the trigger-happy space droids. "Boooo-ah-ah-ah-ahhh. No one can stop the dastardly Villain, mad master of interplanetary bad guys. No one. Boo-ah-ah-ah!" My eerie laughter echoed down the air shafts, sending chills up the spine of every space guard in the quadrant. (A pretty neat trick considering that all the guards were androids—you know, fancy robots.)

As I worked my way down the air shafts toward my hidden space pod, I recalled how I had gotten into this fix in the first place. I'd been busy doing my usual cosmic crime stuff throughout fourteen star systems (talk about overworked!): hijacking Diamel freighters on the planet Zirconia, pillaging spice mines on the planet Paprika, stealing the sacred singing stones of Jagger Moon . . . not returning an overdue book from the public library in Cleveland. Yes, I was an interplanetary pirate without equal (and without brains, according to the space cops who'd found my prints all over everything).

Finally the Galactic Governing Council sent out an elite group of crime fighters, The Blue Fox Squadron. Their leader was my old rival, Cyborg II. There was even a bounty of two million greckles for my capture (about eight bucks in real money). However, for a Goody Two-Shoes like Cyborg II, the reward didn't matter. No, not to Mr. Good Guy . . . Mr. Straight and Narrow . . . Mr. Mom and Asteroid Pie. He did good deeds just for the sake of doing good deeds—things like helping little old ladies cross the Forbidden Zone. So it was no surprise that he would pursue my highly dangerous self across the universe, risking life and limb for peanuts (unsalted, of course). After all, he was the hero. It was his job to do that kind of thing.

My job was to be an evil space villain. Some job. I mean, the pay and hours were lousy. I was chased night and day, often had to go without sleep, and usually ran dangerously low on fuel (and Twinkies). And nobody ever sent me birthday presents . . . believe me, being a fugitive is a real pain.

Well, one night I fell right into one of Cyborg's clever little traps. I'd stopped at a safety inspection station—you know, where they check for faulty thermal reactors, hydroconverters, and any illegal fruit being taken across the border. When I eased into the station, a trooper approached my craft. He asked for my travel code and flight papers, then wanted to know if I was carrying any melons or mangos. When I handed him my papers, he lifted his visor and looked at me with a steely-eyed stare I knew all too well. It was Cyborg II! Faster than you can say, "Obi-Wan Kenobi," the rest of the Blue Fox Squadron surrounded my ship. Their eyes—and their blasters—were aimed right at me.

There I was, surrounded by fifty of the best crime fighters in the galaxy. Now what? *I thought.* Should I fight to the finish? Create a smoke screen? Try to talk my way out of it?

Then it came to me; it was perhaps the most brilliant scheme I had ever conceived! I slowly lifted my arms into the air. Then through sneering lips I whispered those magic words: "I give up."

You know, sometimes I'm so clever I scare myself.

Next thing I knew I was hauled into space court, yelled at by the space judge, fined seventy-five greckles for the case of melons they found hidden in my trunk, and sentenced to eternity in the Mugsy Moon Rock Institute for the Criminally Clumsy. I'd been there ever since.

Until now, that is. Now I was making my escape. And things were going just as I'd expected them to—rotten.

I ended up crawling around in the stupid air shaft for about an hour trying to find Quadrant Three, where I'd hidden my faithful space pod. No luck. It was still hidden. Then I noticed a flashing light through the grill of a vent up ahead. "Aha! Now we're getting somewhere!" I exclaimed.

Drawing closer, I heard the squawk of a guard droid's two-way radio. I anxiously peered out and saw the mechanical moron pacing back and forth. He obviously had his sensors on the look-out for you-know-who.

Suddenly his radio came alive with an urgent transmission: "This is Blue Fox Leader. Any sign of escaped villain in Quadrant Five?"

"Negative, Blue Fox," the guard responded. "All quiet here."

"Be on your toes," Blue Fox said. "This villain's a sneaky little character."

"Affirmative, Blue Fox. I've got my eyes peeled and my nose to the ground. Over and out."

Well, that sounded painful, even for an android. But it was also enlightening. Not only was every guard in the compound hot on my trail, but Cyborg II and his Blue Fox boys were close. Real close. That put a knot in my stomach the size of Jupiter. One thing was sure: I didn't spell relief "C-Y-B-O-R-G."

Well, if I was in Quadrant Five, then Quadrant Three was

nearby. (I'm great with numbers like that.) However, with a maze of air shafts leading a thousand different directions, Quadrant Three wasn't going to be easy to find. There was one thing that would make that search a little easier, though: the guard's radio. I could use it to pick up on the good guys' chitchat and maybe avoid an unpleasant encounter or two. Besides, if things got really boring, maybe I could tune in on the Cubs' game.

Great. Now for the hard part—getting the radio away from this bucket of bolts. With my luck, it was probably a Christmas present, and he was going to be all sentimental about it and wanna keep it. Of course, I needed it more than he did. I just had to convince him of that. Right. Unfortunately, he was bigger than me. In fact, he was the biggest android I'd ever seen.

But I put all my brainpower into action and came up with a plan. I'd wait for the droid to pass underneath me, crown him on the noggin' with the air-vent grill, then jump down, scoop up his radio and immobilizer-blaster, and be merrily on my way.

The plan worked great—well, except for a few slight catches. Slight catch number one: my finger. I got it caught in the grill. Since the grill weighed as much as yours truly, you can imagine what happened next. We both came crashing down on top of the guard, knocking the mechanical wonder to the floor.

Then came slight catch number two.

The blow knocked the droid down. What it didn't do was knock him out. I'd forgotten one little thing: Droids are machines—you can't knock a machine out. Soooo, it was like hitting a grizzly bear with a horseshoe—the only thing that gets knocked out is its teeth. As he slowly got up, I knew this could *mean some heavy hand-to-hand combat. You know, kung fu, karate, chop suey.*

I decided to take the simplest route. I ran between his legs. I must have really confused his circuits because he started spinning around, trying to see where I'd gone. Every time he turned to find me, I'd run back between his legs. Pretty soon the wires in the droid's neck got wound so tight they snapped. I heard this pop and zing, and he conveniently sank to the ground, a pile of limp metal and fizzling wires.

Ha! And they think I'm brainless.

I scooped up his radio and immobilizer and bounded toward the vent. I chuckled as I crawled up and out of sight. "Assignment Radio Raid" had gone off after all. Okay, so it wasn't exactly what you might call a textbook ambush Rambo-style, but it got the job done.

As I continued to trek through the endless air shafts, I occasionally picked up discussions between troopers in certain quadrant numbers. I was getting closer to finding my space pod—but the radio transmissions showed that Cyborg II was getting closer to finding me, too.

I came to another vent and peered out. There were familiar markings on the wall: Q4S7—Quadrant Four, Sector Seven. All right! One quadrant away. Soon I'd be neatly tucked into my space pod and blasting off to freedom. "Colonel Crater's Fried Chicken, here I come!"

Suddenly, a familiar voice came blasting across the radio: "Cyborg II, this is Blue Fox Leader. Quadrant Four, Sector Seven is secure. Do you copy?"

Yipes! He was right on top of me!

"Roger, Blue Fox. No sign of Creeper yet," Cyborg II answered.

Just then I heard the haunting sound of footsteps echoing through the corridor below. "Keep your eyes peeled, Cyborg II," I heard someone exclaim.

I peeked through the vent and sure enough, there he was, a guard droid in tow, drawing closer with every step. My fear suddenly vanished. Why should I be afraid? This was perfect. He didn't know I was up here. For once I was the hammer, he was the nail. I was the cat, he was the mouse. I was the little kid, he was the sucker—well, you know what I mean.

Lifting the immobilizer, I drew a bead on the droid. I'd nail him first, then Cyborg II. Oh, I'd just wing them. You know, put them out of commission long enough for my escape. I mean, even we wicked space villains have a little heart.

Cyborg II continued waltzing toward me, unaware of my presence. His crazy droid followed him, glancing around and whistling some old tune. I think it was the theme song from The Jetsons. *They were getting closer . . . closer. Cyborg II was in range now. I placed my finger on the trigger and slowly began to squeeze . . .*

Nuts—the rotten guard droid was beginning to sing the lyrics now. I wondered if the immobilizer had a setting for "barbecue." I pulled the trigger back. Click . . . click . . . fizz . . . schweeze *. . . Rats! The blaster was out of blast. As Cyborg II and the droid casually strolled on past, I kept squeezing the trigger, hoping for the best. If that bucket of bolts sang much longer, it might kill me. The faulty phaser just fizzed.*

"*Darned no-account, two-bit blaster,*" *I exclaimed. I tossed it in disgust as the off-key, metallic rendition of* The Jetsons *trailed off in the distance.*

I sat there pondering my next move. Then another radio transmission broke the silence: "Blue Fox Leader, this is Cyborg II. Do you copy?"

"Go ahead, Cyborg II. I copy."

"Sir, we've discovered a small spacecraft in Quadrant Three, Sector Twelve. I think you ought to check it out."

"On my way, Cyborg II. Over and out."

Well, if that wouldn't fry the hair off a wookie. Now, they'd found my space pod. The one I worked on in space prison metal shop for months. (I told the guards I was building a flying toaster.) The one I'd hidden away so carefully so I could use it to escape. Oh well, I really didn't want to escape anyway. I was beginning to like it here. Pleasant surroundings. Courteous staff. Fine dining. Yeah, right.

I made a mad dash down the air shaft (as mad a dash as you can make crawling on bony knees). I crawled so fast, I wore holes in the knees of my prison fatigues. Hey, at least I was in style now.

I hoped to reach my space pod in time to spoil Blue Fox's party. I reached the air vent in Quadrant Three and hesitantly took a peek below. I was too late.

Cyborg II was milling about my beloved pod as another Blue Fox trooper came up.

"What is it?" the trooper asked.

"The Creeper's space pod. Set your immobilizers on 'massacre'! We'll destroy the thing before he can put it to use!"

Phasers on "massacre," I thought. Um, I guess they're not kidding around. My only hope was that the pod, made of pure titanium steel, would withstand the phaser blast. If it didn't, I was going to need a lot of duct tape and superglue.

The Blue Fox boys began an all-out assault on my tiny spacecraft. I had to admit I was pleased to see they weren't doing much damage. Their phaser blasts bounced off like tennis balls. Then, just as I decided my ship was going to survive, Cyborg II thew down his blaster in frustration and gave the pod a good swift kick.

BONK! *The little spacecraft shattered into a million useless little pieces.*

"Drat. Lousy, two-bit, no-account titanium," I said. Oh, sure, the stuff can withstand a fifty-megaton explosion. But give it a little punt, and crunch—it goes to pieces on you.

Well, I was done for. Clobbered! Slaughtered! Trashed! Kicked! Whipped! Annihilated! Hammered! You get the idea. It didn't matter, though. After all, it was all just in fun.

Oh, didn't I tell you? This wild galactic battle was just imagination. Yup! In fact, the whole thing had taken place in my little buddy Nick's front yard, not in the far reaches of outer space.

As for my titanium space pod, well, I guess you could say it was actually a pigskin-covered football. The proton blasters? Harmless little toy guns. The maze of air shafts I've been crawling through . . . well, that was simply the old drain gutter that goes down the side of the house. Even the victorious Cyborg II and Blue Fox boys were none other than Nick and his pal, Louis.

Get the picture?

Now before you get all excited and upset, think it over. A make-believe mission is much better than a real one. No one ever gets hurt, and the clean-up expenses after a battle are almost nil. In fact, there is really only one drawback—getting stuck playing the villain. I mean, basically the villain is a real loser. That's okay, though. Who wants the bad guys to win anyway?

Besides, if you play your cards right, even the villain can have a small victory once in a while.

Like thinking up a neat little trick to end the game in your favor.

"A valiant effort, earthling," I said to Nick via the walkie-talkie. "But that was only a three-dimensional projection of my pod."

"McGee, that's not fair!" Nicholas shouted. "We creamed you!"

Nick was right . . . but since when do wicked space villains ever play fair?

"Until we meet again," I called. Then I gave him one final laugh. The famous World's-Most-Wicked-Space-Villain cackle: "Boooo-ah-ah-ah-ahhh!"

TWO

NIGHT OF THE BLOOD FREAKS

"Cheater!" Nicholas shouted into his walkie-talkie.

He hated it when McGee did that. Anytime Nick was about to get the upper hand in one of their imaginary games, McGee would suddenly change the rules. Nicholas knew he and Louis had captured the Creeper's space pod fair and square. They'd won! But nooooo. Suddenly the space pod was just a 3-D picture, and Mr. Creeper McGee had disappeared.

It happened all the time, and it always made Nick furious. Oh, well, that was one of the things you had to put up with when a cartoon drawing was your best friend.

Nick and Louis stood over the somewhat flattened football. It had served well as the Creeper's space pod. Now, thanks to their limitless imaginations, it would become something else. Maybe an alien egg about to hatch little alienites or a space slug about to spew space slime or . . . or . . .

"Nicholas, come on in. It'll be getting dark soon." It was Mom, calling from the front porch.

Nicholas frowned. Moms never understood intergalactic warfare. You could be defending the freedom of the entire galaxy . . . but if it was lunchtime, forget it. Mutant invaders could be threatening our gene pools . . . but if you forgot to put on your coat before going out, too bad. And if you had homework? Well, you could kiss any superhero activity good-bye. After all, what was more important? Getting an A on a spelling quiz or saving all humanoid life-forms as we know them?

"Oh, Mom . . . ," Nicholas protested.

"Come in—now!"

Suddenly the galaxy's safety didn't seem quite so important. Maybe it was the way she said, "Now!" In any case, Nick knew she meant business. So with a heavy sigh he started toward the porch.

"Getting dark soon?" Louis taunted with a smirk at Nicholas. He loved to tease Nick about his parents. They seemed to have all sorts of rules Nick had to follow—what he could do, what he couldn't do, what music he could listen to, how many hours of TV he could watch. In short, if it was fun, Louis figured Nick's folks had a rule against it.

The boys raced up the stairs and threw open the door to Nicholas's room.

"I don't know, Nick," Louis said with a laugh as he plopped down on the bed. "On TV, Cyborg's mom always makes him come in when it gets dark."

Nick spun around and fired off a good burst of imaginary neutrons from his proton blaster. Fortunately it was still set on "massacre." Louis grabbed his chest and did one of his better dying routines. It was beautiful. He choked, he gasped, he sputtered. Then, just when you thought it was all over, he gave one last twitch. Nick had to grin. It was a brilliant performance. On a scale of one to ten, this was definitely an eleven.

Laughing, Nick took off his helmet, and Louis reached for the newspaper they'd brought from downstairs.

"Hey, check it out," Louis said as he turned to the movie section. "*Night of the Blood Freaks—Part IV* starts tomorrow. And it's in 3-D."

"No kidding?" Nicholas asked. He crossed over to the bed for a better look.

"Remember last year," Louis asked, "in *Twilight of the Blood Freaks* when he got those guys at the campfire?"

"Uh, no," Nicholas said, clearing his throat slightly. "I didn't see it. My folks wouldn't let me."

"Man, they don't let you do anything."

"Hey, that was a year ago," Nick protested. "I'm a lot older now, all right?"

Louis gave a shrug and looked back to the ad in the paper. It was as gory as the title. "Have you seen the commercial?" he asked.

Actually, Nick couldn't have helped but see the commercial. It had been running on TV for the last couple of days. It was really gross and really stupid—which probably meant the film would be a smash.

"Yeah, I've seen it," Nick said.

The two boys looked at each other. Each knew exactly what the other was thinking. (That was one of the neat things about having a close friend.) Slowly, they each took a breath and started speaking, together, "First there was *Dawn of the Blood Freaks* . . ."

They made their voices as deep and ominous as they could. Slowly they rose from the bed and sat on its edge. Their volume began to grow. "Then, *Day of the Blood Freaks*."

They continued, sounding louder and scarier with each word. "Then, *Twilight of the Blood Freaks*."

They plopped their feet down hard on the floor at exactly the same time. "But now—" slowly they rose to their feet— "as shadows begin to fall, it's . . . *Night of the Blood Freaks!*"

They screamed and groaned at the top of their lungs, their bodies bouncing and jerking out of control. One minute it looked like they were doing Frankenstein. The next, some new dance step. Then they grabbed their throats and began to cough and choke—all the time screaming their lungs out.

Meanwhile, several families on both sides of the Martins' home stopped what they were doing. What was that sound? What was going on? A few even stepped out onto their front porches for a better listen. From all the screaming and shouting, it was pretty obvious that someone was either being tortured or murdered. Maybe both.

But a few neighbors didn't pay any attention to the racket. They knew Nicholas. They knew about his imagination.

When Nicholas and his family had first moved into Grandma's house, they were pretty excited. After all, here was a fantastic Victorian house that was over a hundred years old. Who knew what secrets the attic held? Who knew what was under those creaky floorboards in the hallway? Who knew which loose bricks in the basement could be moved to discover a secret passageway?

These were the things they expected. What they didn't expect were drafty rooms in the winter or cold showers in the morning (whenever the hot-water heater was on the fritz—which was often). Above all, they certainly didn't expect a house without a dishwasher! I mean, this was the twenty-first century, for crying out loud. Surely Grandma would have a dishwasher!

Well, to be honest, Grandma did have a dishwasher. But like everything else in the house it was a "teensy bit on the broken side." And since Dad wasn't famous for being a handyman (well, he was famous—but in the wrong way), they had to wait and bring in a repairman.

Until then, guess whose children got to wash and dry the dishes by hand! Tonight it was Sarah's turn to wash and Nicholas's turn to dry. They had fried chicken with mashed potatoes and gravy. Grandma's favorite. But not Sarah's. It's not that she minded the taste. It was the cleaning up she hated. Especially the gravy. Especially after they let it sit around for half an hour and it had dried into rubbery, crusty gunk. And, as we all know, once gunk dries, it's impossible to scrape off of dishes. Sarah tried—but not without plenty of sighs, whines, and sarcastic comments only a girl going on fourteen can make.

"This is gross," she muttered. "Why do I always get stuck washing on the gunk days?"

She opened the lid to the plastic garbage can and began to chisel at one of the plates. Chicken bones, gravy, and a few hidden green beans bounced and splattered against an empty milk carton.

Whatever, the family dog, was right there, too. Actually, Whatever was mostly Sarah's dog. Nicholas didn't much care for the little fur ball. The critter always seemed to be whining and yapping. Come to think of it, maybe that was why Sarah and Whatever were such good pals—they were so much alike.

Anyway, Whatever was standing off to the side, barking and begging. He always did that when they had chicken. Forget the stewed tomatoes, the liver, the cooked cauliflower. Anytime you'd try to slip a handful of those delicacies under the table to him so your plate looked clean, he was nowhere to be found. Come chicken night, though, you couldn't get rid of the pest.

"Make sure he doesn't get any of those bones," Mom warned Sarah as she headed into the family room.

Sarah sighed—her answer to just about everything these

days. She knew Whatever liked to chew the bones. She also knew that chicken bones cracked and splintered and that if Whatever got any and swallowed them, he might really hurt himself.

She knew all this—but she also knew how much he liked chicken.

At first she was able to ignore him—but the persistent little critter kept sitting there whining and begging with the most pitiful look on his face. Of course, Nicholas thought he always looked pitiful. But this time, he was pitifully pitiful.

The dog kept working on Sarah's emotions. He used every trick in the begging handbook. Droopy eyes. Pathetic whines. Sad sighs. Nick thought it was disgusting. Revolting. The fact that it was exactly what he often did to get his way with his parents never even dawned on him.

Finally, it worked. Sarah gave in.

It wasn't a big piece. Just a chicken wing. And she really didn't "officially" give it to Whatever. She just sort of let it fall on the floor. Then, before she could grab it, he sort of took it and ran off.

Nicholas started to say something (loud enough, of course, for Mom to hear). Then Sarah shot him the old if-you-know-what's-good-for-you-you'll-keep-your-mouth-shut look. Normally that look would be just what Nick needed to make him say something. But having battled the Space Creeper all afternoon, Nick wasn't ready for another fight.

Instead he asked quietly, under his breath, "You sure you want him eating that?"

"Don't sweat it; he loves chicken," she muttered. "One piece isn't going to hurt him. No biggie."

But for Whatever, it was about to become a biggie. A life-and-death biggie . . .

THREE

GROUNDED

The next morning, *Night of the Blood Freaks* was the talk of the school.

They talked about it on the bus. They talked about it at recess. They talked about it at lunch. The lunch talks were the best. Usually, one of the guys would go into great gory detail over what he expected to see. And usually one of the girls would look down at the ketchup dripping off her hamburger . . . and suddenly lose her appetite.

Later in the day, the kids started drawing pictures and passing them around. Dripping fangs here. Crazed, bloodshot eyes there. Of course, Nick drew the best. That was one thing he could do—draw. He'd never been too much into drawing gore. But after a few tries, he was able to get the hang of it. Pretty soon his stuff was as bad as everyone else's.

Even then, though, even as he was drawing the snarling faces and chewed-up victims, a part of him felt kind of uneasy. He wasn't sure how or why . . . but somehow, some way, a part of him knew it was wrong.

It wasn't a big feeling. No shouting voices, no flashing neon signs. Instead, it was kind of a quiet, almost queasy feeling. Some people would call it his conscience. Nick and his folks would say it was God. In any case, if Nick wanted to, he could ignore that feeling. He could let all the excitement and good times drown it out. . . .

And since that's what he wanted, that's what he did. The uneasy feeling disappeared almost as quickly as it had come. He'd pay attention to it some other time. Right now, he was going to go along with the gang. Just for now, he'd let them slap him on the back and tell him how good his gore was.

On the way home everyone was still talking about the film—especially Louis. "The sound track to the movie is by Death Threat!" he exclaimed.

The kids on the bus all nodded in approval. Renee, not to be outdone, threw in her two-cents' worth. "I've seen all the *Freak* movies," she bragged.

"Seen them?" Louis chirped. "You starred in them!"

Everyone laughed. They usually did whenever Louis zinged someone. Renee gave him the usual roll of her eyes. Still, she had to admit he was pretty sharp.

Finally, the bus pulled to a stop and the doors hissed open. "So what do you think?" Louis asked Nicholas as they headed for the door. "Can you make it to the 2:15 matinee tomorrow?"

"It'll be great!" Nicholas exclaimed as they stepped into the bright sunlight.

But Louis couldn't let it go. Here was another chance to razz Nick about his folks. So, of course, being the good friend he was, Louis did just that.

"Think your mom and dad will let you out of the house?" By the twinkle in Louis's eyes Nicholas knew he was only kidding.

Still, Nick had a reputation to keep up. He didn't want Louis to think he was some wimp who always had to check with his folks for permission. So Nicholas took a chance. Or, rather, he took a guess. . . .

"Hey, I can handle my folks. No sweat."

"All right!" Louis high-fived Nick and they headed for their homes.

When Nick threw open the back door to his house, everyone was in a panic. Sarah was running around looking for an empty box. Mom was shouting orders from the hallway. Little sister Jamie sat on the kitchen stool looking very frightened.

"What happened? What's wrong?" Nicholas asked with concern.

Jamie looked at him. She tried to speak, but she could only get out a loud sniff.

"Mom!" Sarah shouted from the basement. "We've got this old apple crate. Will that do?"

"That's fine!" Mom called. "Grab a beach towel and put it in the bottom so he'll be comfortable."

"What's going on?" Nicholas asked louder.

Suddenly Mom came bursting into the room. In her arms was Whatever. But instead of being his usual cheery, obnoxious self, he lay very still and very quiet. Only an occasional whimper escaped him. "It's Whatever," Mom explained. "There's something wrong with his stomach."

"Oh, Mom. . . ." Jamie started to cry.

"It's okay, Pumpkin. The vet will be able to do something. I'm sure of it." Mom tried her best to stay cool and calm. Jamie tried her best to believe her. Even so, from the way Mom raced around the kitchen, it was obvious she was pretty concerned.

"Honey, will you get the door for me?" she said, turning to Nicholas.

"Sure, Mom." He crossed to the door and opened it. "What happened?"

"Sarah!" Mom called.

"Coming!" Sarah's voice was closer as she raced up the stairs.

"I don't know," Mom said in answer to Nick's question. "Maybe he got into some poison. Maybe it's something he ate. I don't know."

Just then Sarah appeared from the stairs with the apple crate and a beach towel. By the look on her face it was pretty obvious she knew what had happened—and by the look she shot Nicholas it was pretty obvious she knew he knew. . . .

The chicken bone.

Jamie was crying louder now. She was trying her best not to. For a seven-year-old she was doing a pretty good job. Still, she was only seven—and seven meant tears.

"Oh, Pumpkin, he'll be okay," Mom said. Then she turned to Sarah. "Fold the towel and set it inside."

Sarah obeyed; then Mom gently lifted Whatever and carefully set him in the box.

"There you go, boy," she said.

The dog looked up and gave a pitiful little whimper. He looked awful.

Sarah's eyes were starting to burn. She bit her lip to hold back her tears.

"Nicholas," Mom said, "Dad should be home any minute. Watch Jamie for me till he gets here."

"Sure."

She gave him a weak little smile as she passed on her way out the door. "Sarah, are you coming?"

Sarah was right behind her. She didn't say a word. She wouldn't even look at Nick. She just stared at the ground and headed out the door.

Nicholas watched silently as they climbed into the car with Whatever and pulled away.

Sarah's voice was crystal clear in his memory: *"Don't sweat it; he loves chicken. One piece isn't going to hurt him."*

After x-raying Whatever, the veterinarian knew the dog had swallowed something. Probably a bone. The doctor wasn't sure whether she'd have to operate or not. Either way, Whatever would have to spend the night.

On the way home in the car, Sarah finally admitted what she had done. "He loves chicken so much," she blurted. "I just couldn't say no."

Mom tried her best to understand, but she was pretty upset. So was Dad when they got home and told him what had happened. How could Sarah be so irresponsible? Didn't she know what the chicken bones could do?

Sarah did know, and she was more than a little sorry. In fact, she was feeling so bad that Mom and Dad decided to go easy on her.

By the time they'd finished dinner, things had cooled down quite a bit. Enough, Nicholas hoped, that he could ask about seeing the movie. The timing couldn't have been better. Sarah was over at the table doing her homework. Mom was in the kitchen finishing cleaning up. Most important, Dad was upstairs. That was the perfect part! That meant that Mom was separated from him . . . alone . . . vulnerable. When the two of them were together, she was always the softer touch. When she was by herself, well, it would be a piece of cake.

Nick started off by playing it cool and nonchalant, like it was nothing. *With any luck*, he thought, *she'll say yes right off the bat*. But this wasn't Nick's lucky day.

"Absolutely not!" she snapped.

The words fell like a death sentence on his ears. "But, Mom . . ."

"Why would you want to go see a gross movie like that anyway?"

"Cause *he's* gross," Sarah shot back from the table. Now it's true that Sarah was feeling pretty bad about her dog. She was feeling pretty crummy about what she had done. But, hey, she was his older sister. She couldn't let a good put-down like that get by her. After all, she did have a reputation to keep up.

"It's not that bad," Nicholas complained to his mom. But her look made it pretty clear that she'd also seen those TV commercials.

So much for that argument. Nick's brain raced until he found another tactic. It wasn't great, and it wasn't very original—but it was all he had, so he used it: "Besides," he stuttered, "everybody's seeing it."

Immediately he could have kicked himself. How could he be so stupid? He'd left himself wide open for the standard parental comeback. Any second those awful dreaded words would be rolling from Mom's lips: "Oh? You mean if everybody jumped off a cliff, you would jump too?"

He had to act and act fast. He'd jump in before she had a chance to use that deadly phrase. He would jump in with his final—and his best—line of attack. He would use all of his cunning, his wisdom, his brilliance.

He would beg.

"Come on, Mom . . . Pleeease . . ."

He gave her his best wide-eyed, puppy-dog look. It was working. He could see she was starting to soften . . . to break. He had her! Now he'd go in for the kill! Now he'd finish her off with—

"Please what?" a voice asked from the kitchen doorway.

Oh no! It was Dad! Where'd he come from? No fair! Foul! Foul! But it was too late. He had come in to grab a soda from the refrigerator, and his timing couldn't have been worse.

"Nicholas wants to go see a movie with Louis," Mom said.

"Sure, why not?" Dad asked as he poked his head in the fridge.

Nick held his breath. This was it. It could go either way. If Dad just didn't ask the other question—the one that always came up when they talked about movies. If he just didn't ask . . .

"What's it rated?" Aargh! He asked it! That was it. Nick was dead. He knew it.

But instead of an answer, everything was silent. Could it be? Could it be that nobody was going to tell? If no one answered, maybe the question would go away. Chances were good. . . . Dad was busy looking for his diet cream soda. . . . Maybe he wouldn't notice he hadn't gotten an answer. If everybody stayed quiet, then maybe, just maybe, Nick could—

"Oh, it's a real classic," Sarah piped up.

Nicholas glared at her and wondered what the penalty was for murdering your sister. Maybe they'd go easy on him. I mean, who would mind one less big-mouth sister in the world?

She wasn't done, either. In fact, she was grinning. At

last her day had meaning: She could go to bed knowing that once again she had ruined Nicholas's entire life. *"Night of the Blood Freaks—Part IV,"* she told their dad, savoring each word.

Slowly Dad straightened up and looked at Nick over the door of the fridge. Nick tried not to let their eyes meet, but it did no good. He looked at his father pitifully, helplessly. "It's in 3-D," he croaked.

"No way. Absolutely not."

"But, Dad . . ." Nick could feel himself starting to get angry.

"Honey," Mom reasoned, "we don't want you filling your mind with that kind of garbage. You know that."

Now they were coming at him from both sides. "But, Mom . . ."

"I told you so." Sarah couldn't resist getting in another good jab.

Frustrated, Nicholas spun around at her and shouted, "Shut up!"

"Nicholas." Dad's voice was anything but pleased.

"Well . . ." Nick was stuttering, looking for the right words. "Why am I always the one who can't do anything?" His voice was getting high and shrill, a good sign he was losing control.

"Nicholas . . . ," Dad warned.

But it was all coming out now, and there was nothing Nick could do to stop it. "Can't do this; can't do that—"

"One more word out of you, young man—"

"It's not fair," Nicholas shouted over his dad. "Everybody else gets to go out—"

"Nichol—" Mom tried to stop him from getting in any worse hot water, but Nick was too busy shouting to hear.

"Everybody else gets to go, but I have to sit around with a bunch of old—"

"That's it!" Dad's voice was sharp and to the point. It immediately brought Nicholas to a stop. He'd gone too far, and he knew it.

Dad continued, firm and even. "We don't talk that way in this home. Now go to your room. You're grounded."

Nicholas couldn't believe his ears. Grounded! How could this have gone so wrong?

He looked at Dad. The man stood solid and firm. Then he looked at his mom. She was also holding her ground.

Nick felt his ears start to burn, his head start to pound. He was so mad he felt like exploding, but what could he do? His dad had spoken. And by the tone in his voice and the look in his eyes, Nick knew he meant every word of it.

Nicholas Martin, Mr. I-can-handle-my-folks-no-sweat, was grounded—and there was nothing he could do about it.

Finally he snapped around and started for the stairs. It was so unfair. All of it!

He reached the bottom of the steps and started to stomp up them—loudly. He might not be able to say anything more, but no one had said anything about stomping.

Mom and Dad looked on. Neither was happy about having to ground Nicholas. Unfortunately, he'd given them no choice.

FOUR

EVERYBODY'S A CRITIC

Parents. Yeah, you know who they are. The folks that hang around your house telling you when to walk, talk, and jump— and how high. The big guys who always hand out orders like "Take out the trash. Eat your vegetables. Take a bath. Practice your tuba. Stop practicing your tuba. Don't pick at it. Change your socks. Clean up your room. Get a haircut . . ." and about a thousand other things that you hate to do.

But, hey, they can't help it. That's their job. Everyone knows parents are supposed to make you do all those things and prevent you from having fun.

Oh, yeah. They're best at that—at preventing you from having fun. Like when you want to go skateboarding down the freeway with Tom, Dick, and Harry. The answer is always no: "No, you'll get run over. Skateboard around the house, where it's safe."

Okay, so it's a pain to stay home while Tom, Dick, and Harry get to skateboard down the freeway. But hey, like I always say, it's easier to stay home than wind up a pancake under some semi's rear tire.

Besides, I've noticed something interesting. Nick's folks usually only put the clamps on him when his "fun" is gonna end up messing him up. I know, it doesn't make being clamped any easier. But I've got a pretty good hunch that's how it is with most parents.

Shucks, parents are bound to know something. I don't think you can get that job unless you've been around and learned some things. Unfortunately, convincing my buddy Nick of that wasn't easy.

Dad and Mom had just dropped the big one on Nick's plans for Night of the Blood Freaks. *He had lost the war—big time. Not only was he forbidden to see the gross-out flick with Louis, but his "diplomacy" had landed him in the clink. He came stomping into the bedroom, mad at the world, just as I was getting ready for bed and brushing my teeth.*

I decided to take pity on my pal, maybe enlighten him on the workings of parent-child relationships. Of course, this meant I was going to have to think like an adult. Not an easy task, but I figured I'd give it a shot.

As Nick wrestled with his shirt and kicked off his shoes, I began my approach. "Hey, Nick," I started off cheerfully.

"Ah, go smell your socks," he barked.

"Wound a bit tightly tonight, aren't we?" I kidded.

But he just kept yanking his clothes off as if they were on fire and sank into the bed in a boiling heap of frustration.

"Look, kid," I said, trying to reason with him. *"You watch movies like that long enough, and pretty soon they'll stick a sign on your head that says 'Dump Site.'"*

"What are you, some kind of film critic?" he scoffed as he tucked back the covers and crawled into bed.

"Well, as a matter of fact . . ."

Suddenly we were seated in a deserted theater balcony (ain't imagination grand?). I was crammed into a snug-fitting V-neck sweater and an equally tight pair of polyester slacks. Nick was in an open-collar dress shirt and a well-fitting navy blazer. We had become the Dynamic Duo of movie criticdom: Roger Beefer and Gene Dismal, the cohosts of TV's Let's Mangle the Movies.

"Well, Gene," I said, *"let's take a look at our next clip,* The Molting Falcon. *Okay, roll it."* Nothing happened. *"Roll it! Roll it already!"*

Finally the screen began to flicker, and the movie began. · . .

"My name is Shade," the leading man said (an outstanding, award-winning actor who bore an uncanny resemblance to yours truly). *"Spam Shade, Private Eye. I was relaxing in my second-story office on the lower East Side: the lower, lower East Side. It was so low the snails wore elevator shoes just to stay on the sidewalks. Even so, it wasn't as low as I was feeling.*

"I was down. I had been working two weeks, night and day, on a case that was really a tough nut to crack. (Actually, it was a

walnut. I'd used a hammer, a pair of pliers, and a screwdriver, and I still hadn't gotten the thing open. A guy could starve to death. Next Christmas I hoped Aunt Nellie would send me a fruitcake instead.) I sat back in my chair and took a stout swig of my diet soda.

"Then she walked in.

"She stepped into the place like she owned the joint. She leaned against the doorway and drew out a cigarette. I guess she didn't notice the No Smoking sign. Being a gentleman, I was gonna offer her a light. Then I saw she had one. A blow torch.

"She lit up the room. As a matter of fact, she lit up the coatrack. We put the fire out; then I asked her her name. 'Thelma,' she said. She was the kind of babe your mom warned you about. That's okay, though. Mom was in Cleveland getting a nose job. So I asked Thelma to take a seat.

"She sat down, then said she was looking for her bird, a molting falcon. She whipped out a half-charred photo and handed it to me. It was a picture of her and the bird standing in front of Old Geezer, the world famous waterspout in Yellow Phones National Park. The bird was wearing a polka-dot tie. It looked like they had been on vacation. . . . I was beginning to think they were also out to lunch.

"Thelma said the bird had disappeared around the docks. She thought the whole thing smelled kind of fishy. I wondered what she expected the docks to smell like.

"Well, it just so happened I had been down at the docks earlier and found just such a bird. I whipped it out of my drawer. The tie matched, and so did the bird. Too bad it was dead now.

"Just then I heard a blood-curdling scream accompanied by a loud thud. It was Thelma, passed out on the floor. I guess she was the sensitive type. Either that or it was time for her afternoon nap.

"Oh well, that wraps up another thrilling case for Spam Shade, Private Eye."

The lights in the theater came up, and I turned to my partner. "You know, Gene," I said, "they just don't make films like that anymore. Great story, great dialogue—and a particularly great performance by the lead. I give this flick a thumbs-up."

"No way," Roger said. "If that film was any flatter, it would be in the House of Pancakes. Now if you want to see a really great flick, let's take a look at the new remake, starring that action-packed performer, Flint Streethood. Okay, roll it."

Now, folks, as near as I can tell, this film had something to do with somebody being mad at somebody about something, and it's just as well you never see it. Still, let me see if I can describe what happened.

Some guy carrying a gun the size of a B-52 bomber walked into a drugstore and said, "Okay, punk, make my parfait." The next thing I know, everybody was shooting at everybody else. It went something like this:

Kapow! Kapow! Blam! Blam! Whir! Bang! Bang! Bang! Rat-tat-tat-tat-tat-tat-tat-tat! Kaboom! Kawham! Bang! Cough! Cough! Kak-kak-kak-kak! Wheeze! Wheeze! Kagang! Kagang! Whir! Whir! Pop!

Are you getting the idea? The last thing I remember was a grenade coming straight out of the screen and—KaWHOOM!

"You call that fun?!" I gasped. The blast had blown us clear out of our make-believe theater and back to the bedroom—which was fine with me. "Why don't you just stick your head in a garbage can?"

"Because then I would have to room with you," Nick said with a cough as he reached for the light next to the bedpost. "Let's just try to get some sleep."

Well, at least he's forgotten about the silly *Blood Freak* flick, *I thought.* Then again, who knows? Tomorrow is another day, and boys will be boys. Or will they?

FIVE

CYBORG'S PLAN

By 9:00 the next morning, things had started to look a little better. Not perfect, mind you, but a little better. For starters, it was Saturday. And Saturday meant, you guessed it, no school! It's not that Nicholas hated school. It's just that he could think of a lot better ways to spend six hours a day, which according to his calculations meant,

6 hours x 5 days = 30 hours a week!

30 hours x 4 weeks = 120 hours a month!

120 hours x 9 months = 1,080 hours a year!

1,080 hours a year in school! Awful! Terrible! Of course, Nick ignored the fact that the only reason he could do those calculations was because he had spent so much time in school.

Anyway, another reason Saturday morning looked better was that Nick had cooled down some. As usual, his talk with McGee had helped. Not that he agreed with the little munchkin. Hardly. But he was able to understand a little more where his folks were coming from. Only a little, though.

Another good thing was the news on Whatever. The vet called bright and early that morning to say that everything was fine. There was no need to operate. In fact, they could pick him up anytime they wanted.

Of course, Sarah had her dad talked into going down there in no time flat. She was feeling pretty good. In fact, she was feeling so good that she started to make excuses about giving Whatever the bone. They were barely out of the garage before she had herself convinced that it wasn't even her fault.

"I was just doing the loving thing," she insisted. "You couldn't expect me to be some old ogre and say no, could you? I mean, not when I love him?"

Dad could only shake his head at her logic. "It's because you love him that I'd expect you to say no," he explained.

Sarah looked at him, confused.

"Sweetheart," he continued, "just because you love someone doesn't always mean you let him have his way. I mean, look at Nicholas."

"I'd rather not," she cracked.

Dad ignored the comment. "Nick wanted to see that movie—but we knew it was bad for him."

"You mean with all the blood and gore and junk?"

"Right. Seeing that movie would be as bad for Nick's mind as that chicken bone was for Whatever's stomach."

"Okay . . . so . . ."

"So," Dad continued, "which would have shown him more love? Letting him go off and do something that would hurt him, or saying no and letting him be angry at us?"

"I guess saying no."

Dad nodded.

Sarah was starting to see the picture . . . and for once she didn't have a comeback. Well, she always had a comeback. This one just wasn't great. "It's hard to say no," she insisted. "I mean, you know how Whatever loves chicken."

"It's hard for us to say no to you guys, too. If we had it our way, we'd always say yes. We'd always give you what you wanted. But we see the bigger picture, and because we love you . . . well, sometimes we have to be the heavy and say no."

Sarah looked out the window. After a long moment, she said, "Being a parent doesn't always sound so easy."

"No kidding!" Dad exclaimed.

Sarah turned back to him and grinned. "It has its rewards, though, doesn't it?"

A puzzled look came across her dad's face. "Well," he said, "if you hear of any, let me know."

"Daddy!" Sarah gave him a poke in the ribs, and he broke into a grin.

It's too bad Nicholas hadn't heard that conversation. Maybe his decision would have been different when Louis called. . . .

"Hello?"

"Hey, Nick." Louis's voice was a little thick and raspy from the morning, but Nicholas immediately recognized it. "You ready for the flick?"

Oh no, Nick thought. He'd forgotten all about his promise to Louis. Not only would he have to explain why he couldn't go, but now he'd have to go through all of Louis's jabs and jokes about how strict his parents were. To make it worse, his mother was standing three feet away at the kitchen sink. Well, better to get it over with, quick and simple. . . .

"I can't go."

"What?" Louis asked.

"I'm grounded."

"Grounded?" Louis knew Nick's parents were strict—but not that strict. "How are you going to the movie if you're grounded?"

"I can't."

"Oh, man. . . . " Louis sighed.

It wasn't easy for Mom to hear this conversation. She knew how important the movie was to Nick. She could tell how embarrassed he was. Still . . . she also knew how rude he'd been the night before. Even more important, she knew how harmful the movie would be.

Unfortunately, the wheels inside Louis's brain were turning. An idea was coming to his beady little brain. "Hold it. Wait a minute," he said. "Wait a minute . . . 'Blue Fox Leader?'"

"Huh?" Nick didn't get it. What did the TV series have

to do with his being grounded? How was that going to help him see the movie?

"Remember last week's episode?" Louis asked. "Remember the plan Cyborg II used to free Blue Fox Leader from the dreaded Black Tower?"

It took Nicholas a moment to catch on. Then he remembered the show . . . he remembered how Cyborg and Blue Fox used their telecommunicators, how Cyborg distracted the Scorpion-tailed android guards so Blue Fox could make his escape. Most important, he remembered how Blue Fox used his superior creativity to build a decoy.

"Superior creativity. Hmmmmm." That was right up Nicholas's alley. He cast a guarded look at his mom and slid out of earshot as he and Louis worked out their plan. . . .

First Nick attached the toilet plunger.

It took some doing, but with superglue and the right amount of suction, Nick was able to make it stick onto the inside of his bedroom door.

Next came the electrical cable. Sure, it looked like a lot of twisted-up Christmas tree lights. And he probably didn't need them all blinking. But, hey, that was part of the effect. He hooked one end of the cable to a small sensor on the plunger. Then he attached the other end to a tape recorder on his bed.

Now for the recorded message. Nick was careful to make his voice sound just bored enough.

For the normal kid, this stuff would be pretty hard

to do. Nicholas, however, was no normal kid. He had this imagination that just wouldn't stop. You could see it in all of his McGee drawings. You could see it in his automatic walnut cracker. You could see it in his light-activated door opener. Today, though, he'd outdone himself. Today he'd created the fool-your-parents-so-they-think-you're-still-in-your-room invention.

The last step was the lightbulb. He screwed it into the socket attached to the plunger. Then Nick hesitated for a moment. This was it. Would it really work? He took a deep breath and gently knocked on the door.

The bulb lit! It was a success! All right!

It had taken him nearly two hours. Two hours of rummaging for parts in the garage, the basement, the attic . . . and then there were all those delicate electrical hookups. Finally, though, he was finished. And it actually worked!

Just in time, too. Almost immediately his walkie-talkie began to beep. It had to be Louis.

Nicholas picked it up and said, "Cyborg II, this is Blue Fox Leader. Do you copy?"

For a moment there was no answer, and Nick's heart began to sink. Without Louis the plan would not work. Without Louis he couldn't possibly sneak out. Without Louis—

"Roger, Blue Fox. I'm reading you loud and clear."

Nick broke into a grin.

Louis was outside, hiding in the front yard. He was trying his best to look like the superintelligent and ever-so-wise Cyborg II. Unfortunately, he didn't quite make it.

Maybe it was his clothes. Maybe it was the pulled-down stocking cap, the thick scarf, and the heavy sweatshirt. Or maybe it was all the sweat he was covered with from wearing those clothes in the eighty-degree weather. In any case, Louis looked more like a crazed bag lady than the all-knowing hero from Kalugrium.

That didn't stop him, though. Not one bit. Fantasy was fantasy, and he planned to play this one to the hilt.

"Synchronize watches to 11:28," Louis continued, "and let's commence execution."

"Execution?" The word caught Nicholas off guard. Until now it had all been fun and games; it really hadn't been real . . . but "execution" sounded an awful lot like punishment. And punishment would definitely be part of Nick's future if he were caught. After all, he was disobeying his parents—and in a *big* way.

Reality only lasted a second, though. Louis soon brought Nick back to his senses.

"Yeah. Execute the plan. You know, 'the plan.'"

"Oh, uh, right . . . the plan."

Nicholas grinned as he pushed down the antenna and threw on his coat. Everything was going great! Everything had been worked out. There would be no problems.

Or so he thought . . .

Tsk, tsk, tsk . . . "What a tangled web we weave when we prac-i-tac-tice to deceive." That's what I always say. And that's exactly what my good buddy Nick was doing. He thought he was being quite the clever escape artist with all those electronic gizmos and wires running every which way.

I must admit his creativity in the matter was quite impressive. His electronic doodads gave a realistic impression that he was calmly sketching in his room. Well, everybody else might be fooled, but not me.

I don't know. It seemed like a lot of wasted effort to fool his parents just so he could go and be grossed out. Why didn't he just go downstairs and make a broccoli and stewed prune sandwich? Always works for me.

Besides, seems to me Nick should devote his time to more rewarding activities. You know, challenging endeavors that would spark his mind and spirit. Things that would help him be a better person. Things like . . . well, you know . . . like clipping his toenails.

Yeah. That's it. If he would clip his toenails on a regular basis, it would . . . well, it would . . . Okay, it wouldn't do anything. But since it was what I was doing at the time, I thought it was pretty worthwhile.

Still, as preoccupied with that task as I was (after all, I didn't want to cut off my big toe or something), I decided it was time to tell Nick how I felt about his little rendezvous with Louis. "You'll be sorry," I said, continuing to trim away at my tootsies.

"Aren't you coming?" Nick asked.

Obviously, he knew if I played along with his clever little scheme, he'd have a better chance of pulling it off. But I didn't want any part of it. "Uh-uh, no way," I said in a superior tone.

"*I got principles. I got convictions.*" *I leaped to my feet and began to sing, "I got rhythm . . ."*

But Nick wasn't the least bit impressed. He just stood there for a second, until a sly grin crossed his face. He had an idea, I could tell. But it wouldn't work. No matter what he said, I was going to make him realize how I felt about this whole underhanded plot. Nothing was going to change my mind. So I just kept on singing, "I got rhythm . . ."

"I'll give you a dollar," he offered.

"I got . . . to get my shoes," I said.

Okay, so I gave in. Can I help it if I was flat busted and would do anything for a buck? Well, at least I'll have a little walking money for the movie, *I thought. Although all you can get at the movies for a buck these days is a cup of ice and half a Milk Dud.*

Nick made some final adjustments on his fool-your-folks invention while I laced up my glow-in-the-dark tennis shoes. (I like to see where I'm walking in those dark theaters.)

We both stood there a second, took a deep breath, then cautiously crept out of the bedroom.

I sure hoped this stupid plan worked. Or we would end up in worse shape than any of the victims in this freak flick ever thought about.

SIX

THE ESCAPE!

Carefully Blue Fox ("Nick" to his friends) moved down the stairs. Who knew where his enemies lurked? Who knew what dastardly tortures he would face if caught? It didn't matter, though, for his courage was great. Yes, the courage of Blue Fox Leader was beyond compare.

Unfortunately, there was only one way out—through the Control Center of the enemy's fortress (which, to untrained eyes, looks a lot like a kitchen).

Thanks to months of training, Blue Fox knew exactly which steps creaked and which didn't. With expert wisdom he avoided those hidden alarms, which had obviously been placed by enemies to alert them in case he tried to escape.

As he approached the Control Center, he could hear the murmur of an alien voice. With each step the voice grew louder. By its higher pitch, Blue Fox could tell it was the Female Unit, the second in command. Fortunately, the Supreme Commander was out back spray painting some patio furniture.

Carefully Blue Fox peeked around the corner of the stairs. There she was . . . the Female. She was talking on the phone to the counseling center. Across the counter in the family room, Blue Fox could see the Female Unit's mother. They called her Grandma for short. She had her back to him and was knitting. Probably some phaser-proof vest for one of the Offspring.

Ah, yes. The Offspring!

Quickly Blue Fox scanned the area. Fortunately the Offspring were nowhere to be found. Good. Well, good and bad. Good because it meant Blue Fox would not have to sneak past them. (The Offspring's senses were much keener than those of the Older Units.) Bad because the Offspring were just the kind of creatures who would suddenly swoop in from nowhere and catch him out in the open.

This was not a time for fear, though. This was a time for action. Blue Fox knew he had to cross the Control Center. That meant the Female Unit must be removed. Blue Fox pulled back out of sight. Quickly he keyed in his telecommunicator.

"Cyborg II, Cyborg II, this is Blue Fox Leader," he whispered. "Emergency at kitchen. Request diversionary tactics."

Louis was still outside hiding in the front yard when his buddy's call for help came. All right! This was what he'd been waiting for! He answered, "Roger, Blue Fox. I'm on my way."

Like a shot, he jumped up from behind the concrete wall and headed for the front porch. It was a dangerous mission. Any moment he could be spotted by the enemy and demolecularized (you know, melted into a little puddle of loose atoms). That didn't matter, though, because that was his friend in there. That was the great Blue Fox Leader. And if there was one thing Cyborg II was famous for, it was his loyalty.

Inside, Blue Fox pressed himself flat against the stairway wall and waited. Would Cyborg II complete his mission?

It had been tricky, and Cyborg II had had more than one close call. Finally, though, he reached the stairs of the front porch. Just in time, too, for a motorized vehicle (that earthlings would call a "car") came racing around the corner. Cyborg II dropped behind the bushes out of sight as it passed.

Then, summoning all his strength and courage, Cyborg II rose from hiding, glanced about, and raced up the stairs toward the front door, where he reached out and rang the doorbell . . . once, twice. Then he darted down the steps as quickly as he had come.

When he heard the doorbell, Blue Fox grinned, Cyborg II had not let him down. Furthermore, the plan had the desired effect upon the Female Unit.

"Uh, Mary Ann?" the Female Unit said into the phone. "Can you hold on? There's somebody at the door."

Blue Fox heard her set the phone down on the counter and push open the hallway door. Perfect!

Now it was time to make his move!

He started across the kitchen, planning to go through the family room and out the other door. With any luck he'd go completely undetected.

So much for luck . . .

"Sarah . . . ," he heard the Female Unit call from the hallway. "Can you see who that is at the door?" Then the hallway door started to open.

Oh no! What should he do!? The Female Unit was coming back in, and he was trapped out in the open! Then he spotted it—the control console, cleverly disguised as one of those stove tops built in the middle of the kitchen. It wasn't very big, but it would have to do. He dove for cover just as the door opened.

Blue Fox held his breath, waiting. He was crouched on one side of the little kitchen island, and the Female Unit was standing on the other. They were less than four feet apart.

She picked up the phone and started talking again. For a moment, Blue Fox was safe. Well, not quite. True to form, the Female Unit liked to keep busy. There was a long cord on the phone, so she could move all around the kitchen as she talked.

Suddenly Blue Fox heard her approaching footsteps. Oh

no! She was heading right for him! Quickly he scrambled on his hands and knees to the opposite side.

He made it just as she rounded the corner. It was close, but he was safe.

Suddenly the Female Unit changed directions and headed the opposite way. Blue Fox frantically switched into reverse and backed up. Then she changed directions again, and so did he. It looked like some strange sort of dance as she unknowingly chased him around the little island . . . first one direction, then the other, and then the first direction again.

Blue Fox Leader was beginning to feel a little ridiculous . . . not to mention a lot dizzy.

Finally the Female Unit finished her conversation and hung up the phone. Then Blue Fox Leader heard it . . . that wonderful sound of the squeaky kitchen door being opened again.

"Sarah?" the Female Unit called. "Sarah, who was at the door?"

Perfect! She was out of the room. Blue Fox rose to his feet and started for the family room door, only to dive again for cover as the Offspring threw it open. "Mother?"

Now Blue Fox Leader was at the end of the kitchen counter—the one that separated the kitchen from the family room. And if that wasn't bad enough, Female Unit suddenly came back through the kitchen door. "Oh, there you are."

What is this, a convention? Blue Fox thought. It was crazy. The Female Unit was on one side of the counter, and the Offspring was on the other. While he, the great Blue Fox

Leader, was trapped in between. All either of them had to do was cross three feet down his way, and bingo, they'd spot him.

"Who was at the door?" the Female Unit asked.

"No one," the Offspring answered.

"Probably one of those silly kids."

"But, Mom," the Offspring cracked. "Nicholas is upstairs."

For a moment Nick thought it was unfair that the real Blue Fox Leader didn't have to put up with a sister.

"Grandma?" The Offspring turned toward the sofa, where the Older Unit sat. "Can you help me with the curtains in my room?"

"Well, sure, dear," the Older Unit answered.

Blue Fox heard the creak of the sofa as she rose to her feet. "How do they look?" she asked. "Is the length okay?"

Great! They were heading toward the door.

"Well, kind of," the Offspring answered. "But it's uneven at the bottom."

"We'll take care of that," the Older Unit said as the door creaked open and their voices faded down the hall.

Super! Now it was just Blue Fox and the Female Unit!

He leaned back and looked over his shoulder. She was at the counter starting to make some peanut-butter-and-jelly nutrition packets. Silently he dropped to his knees and inched his way around to the family room side of the counter.

The doorway lay just ahead. All he had to do was quietly crawl toward the door. . . .

Carefully he crept forward. Foot by foot, inch by inch. All the time he could hear the Female Unit just above his head, on the other side, preparing the meal. Closer and closer the door came. He was nearly there.

A good thing, too. The game was starting to wear on Nicholas. It had started off fun enough, but all this sneaking, this hiding, this disobeying . . . well, it was definitely starting to take its toll on him. A tight knot of guilt had started growing in his stomach, and it was growing bigger by the second.

Finally he reached his hand out to the door. Soon it would be over. Then the worst happened. He was spotted—by a four-legged hair ball. It was the Offspring's pesky pooch! And worse yet, the carnivorous canine thought Blue Fox wanted to play. So he began to bark.

Blue Fox tried to shush him. He tried to silence him. The animal just took it as a sign of encouragement. He'd just spent the last twelve hours at the vet's, teetering between life and Poochie Paradise. Now that he was okay, he figured it was time to party.

"What on earth?" the Female Unit leaned over the counter toward the dog. She was directly above Blue Fox's head but could not see him. "Whatever—are you all right, boy?"

The dog continued to bark.

"Whatever . . . what's wrong, fella?" Her voice sounded more concerned.

Oh no! Any minute she'd set down her knife and cross into the family room to check out the problem. Maybe she thought he was still sick. Maybe she thought he was having a relapse. Either way, once she crossed around the counter, she would spot the great Blue Fox Leader!

Desperately, Blue Fox looked for a solution. Anything—he'd even settle for a chicken bone right now. There was nothing.

Well . . . almost nothing. . . .

Have you ever noticed this? That in the most critical moment of a daring and dangerous escape plan, when the safety of the entire free world rides on split-second timing, there's always some mangy mutt hanging around who starts barking his head off? Which, of course, alerts everyone from Cleveland to Crabwell Corners of your presence. Have you ever noticed that?

It happens every time. In fact, it was happening right now to my good buddy, Nick.

Whatever, the family fur ball, was only seconds away from blowing our movie mission. The half-witted hound's persistent barking had to go; otherwise Nicholas would probably replace this pooch in the doghouse.

What old Rover needed was a little game of fetch, commando style. I whipped out a nice, round, black bomb, which I keep for such occasions, and lit the fuse. Nick gave me a look of alarm. I think he was afraid I was about to give this pup a permanent toothache. Of course, that wasn't the plan.

I gave Nick a reassuring wink, then beckoned to Whatever with the burning bomb. "Come here, boy," I called, slapping my thigh and giving a soft whistle, waving the bomb around like a fine turkey bone.

The dorky dog stopped barking and stepped forward hesitantly. Hooray for curiosity.

I continued to sweet-talk the critter, until he finally sniffed at the fizzing fuse. Just as I had hoped, a spark flew out and smacked Whatever right on the nose. The chickenhearted cat chaser turned tail and raced through the kitchen and up the stairs, yelping all the way.

Mom, somewhat startled, dropped what she was doing and followed in hot pursuit. "Whatever, are you okay? Come here. Come here, fellow. Whatever?"

Nick heaved a sigh of relief. "Thanks," he whispered.

I licked my fingers and pinched out the burning fuse. "It will cost you another seventy-five cents," I said calmly.

Nick looked annoyed. But, hey, that had been a pretty desperate situation. Besides, the extra cash would come in handy at the movie. Now I could get a whole Milk Dud.

Nick rose to his feet, shot a glance around the room, then crept out of the kitchen. "Let's go," he whispered to me over his shoulder.

This movie had better be worth it, *I thought as I followed him out of the kitchen.* Or I'm going to charge him another quarter when we get home.

By the time Nick made it outside, he was exhausted. All that sneaking around had worn him out. Besides, that little knot of guilt in his stomach was now about the size of a baseball. Needless to say, he was glad the game was finally over.

Well, almost.

Louis was still wearing his stocking cap. His scarf was still pulled up over his face, and he was still using their walkie-talkie. Nick may have been done with the game, but Louis had only begun.

"C'mon," Louis whispered. "Follow me."

Nicholas glanced around. "Why are we whispering?"

"Shhhh."

Louis turned—and fell over the garbage cans beside them. They clanked and rattled and banged, making all sorts of racket. Some of the neighborhood dogs started barking.

The two boys pressed flat against the wall just as Mom stuck her head out the front door to have a look. She saw nothing.

"Strange," she said as she finally turned to shut the door. "Very strange."

The boys relaxed, but Nick's heart was beating like a jack-hammer. Louis glanced around, then turned to Nicholas and whispered, "Meet me over by that Buick."

"Louis," Nicholas said with a sigh. "Let's just go to the theater." He was sick of the game . . . and he was sick of all the guilt he was feeling.

"What are you talking about?" Louis demanded. "That's not what Blue Fox would do."

"No, and Blue Fox's mom wouldn't chase him around the kitchen, either."

"Let's just stick to the plan," Louis urged. With that he dashed off.

Nicholas swallowed hard. He wanted to be a good sport, but he also wanted to get rid of the guilt he was feeling. I mean, here his folks were trusting him, expecting him to obey . . . and look what he was doing. It felt terrible. That ball lying in his stomach was now the size of a volleyball. He took a deep breath, muttered something about not remembering a Buick in the plan, and finally took off.

SEVEN

ATTACK OF THE BLOOD FREAKS

The boys had plenty of time to walk to the theater. But superheroes never walk. They dash, dart, or zip. So Louis made sure they did just that . . . all the way.

By the time they finally reached the theater, Nicholas wasn't sure if the pain in his gut was from the guilt or from all the running. Either way, it felt bad. And it was getting worse.

Finally, there it was. The theater. And up on the marquee, in glorious dripping red, was the title: *Night of the Blood Freaks—Part IV.*

Nicholas swallowed hard. He had come this far. There was no backing out now. Then a thought struck him.

"Wait a minute, Louis," he said. "How are we supposed to get in if we're not old enough?"

Not to worry. The great Cyborg II had already figured out a plan. "No problem," he said with a grin. "Follow me." With that, he took off for the ticket line.

Nicholas swallowed again. By this time, though, there wasn't much left to swallow. His mouth was as dry as the Sahara desert. Numbly, he turned and followed his friend to the back of the line.

Interestingly enough, the back of the line doesn't stay the back of the line forever. Nick saw that they were moving closer and closer toward the box office window. Any second they'd be there. Any second Nick's crime would be found out. Any second SWAT teams would appear, arrest him, and throw him in jail for life. Or, worse yet, he'd be forced to listen to one of his dad's lectures.

Closer and closer they came. Why had he agreed to this? What had he been thinking of?

Now the man in front of them stepped up to the window. He was average looking—Greek or maybe Arab. Not a bad sort of fellow. He paid for his ticket and moved off.

It was their turn.

Nicholas looked up to the box office attendant. She was kind of pretty, but he didn't notice. He was paralyzed. He couldn't move. He couldn't speak.

Fortunately, Louis could. And he did. Beautifully. "Two, please," he said. Then, turning to the man who had just left, he called out, "Wait up . . . Dad."

A stroke of genius! A brilliant plan! In one sentence Louis had solved all of their problems. Those three little words would get them in, free and clear. Fantastic! Except for one minor problem—"Dad" was Greek; Louis was black.

The box office attendant frowned down at them. Always thinking, Louis pointed to Nicholas. "His dad," he said, reaching in to grab the tickets and head after the man.

"Whew, that was close," Louis whispered to Nicholas . . . but Nicholas was not there. He was still frozen in front of the box office, a pathetic little smile pasted on his face.

Louis took a step back, grabbed him by the collar, and yanked him toward the door.

Back at home, Mom was feeling pretty proud of her son. Nick had taken his punishment so well. He really was a wonderful kid. Not one word of complaint from him all morning. In fact, she hadn't heard any word from him for several hours. She decided to swing up to his room and say hi and tell him how proud she was of him. Then maybe, just maybe, the whole family could get out later and do something together. Maybe pizza. Maybe miniature golf. Maybe both.

She knocked gently on his door and waited.

Her "wonderful" son's little invention—the one he had spent so much time hooking up—finally went into operation.

Mom's knock started it all by lighting up the light on the door. This sent electricity down the long cable of Christmas tree lights to the tape recorder. The power snapped the recorder on "play," and suddenly Mom heard Nick's voice recorder loud and clear: "Who is it?"

"It's Mom," she said from the other side.

"I'm drawing right now," Nick's voice said. "Could you come back later?"

"All right, hon," Mom said, and she left his door with a smile.

What a terrific kid. Other children might have sulked or stayed mad. Not Nicholas. He took his medicine like a real trouper. What a kid. What a delight.

Mom moved down the hall beaming with pride.

Well, Nicholas was taking his medicine all right. Just not exactly the way Mom thought.

At first things in the theater were okay. Nick had never worn 3-D glasses before, and it was pretty exciting the way the credits seemed to jump off the screen at him. For a few moments the ache in his gut was almost gone, and he was actually glad he'd come.

Then the movie started.

The slimy, half-rotted mutants weren't so bad to look at. In fact, it was kind of fun to watch the way they hobbled across the lawn. And their slurping, sucking noises were more disgusting than scary. It was when they got into the house . . . and what they did to their first victim . . . well, at first it was kind of interesting. Then it got gross. Then more gross. Then, when you were sure it couldn't get any more gross . . . it did.

Nick glanced at Louis. It was hard to see his friend's expression behind those 3-D glasses. Still, Louis was definitely feeling something. I mean, the kid was munching down popcorn faster than Nick had ever seen him eat in his life.

Now the Freaks were starting up the stairs of the house—heading up to find the rest of the family.

It had been nearly half an hour since Mom checked in on Nicholas. She had just gone upstairs to put away laundry, so she figured she'd stop by and give another knock.

"Who is it?" the recorded voice asked. Only this time it started to drag, which made Nick's voice sound very low and slow. Apparently, Nick had forgotten one small element in his perfect plan: He hadn't checked the batteries in the tape player.

Mom frowned. "Honey, it's Mom. Are you okay? You sound . . ."—she searched for the right word—"tired."

No answer.

"Nicholas?"

She knocked again.

Still no answer.

"Nicholas?" Her concern started to grow. She knocked harder, which shook the cable attached to the recorder, which made the delicate little connectors shake loose and short out—which tripped the tape player into "record" mode.

"Nicholas, it's Mom. What's going on in there?" More knocking. More shaking. The recorder clicked back into "play" mode.

Finally, Mom heard an answer from the other side of the door—but not the one she was expecting. "It's Mom," the voice said. "What's going on in there?"

Mom stopped a moment. That sounded like *her* voice. Not only did it sound like her voice—it *was* her voice.

Sarah stuck her head out of her room to see what the fuss was about. "Hey, Mom, what're you doing?"

They looked at each other. Something was wrong. Something was definitely wrong.

That did it. Mom turned the knob and threw open the door. "Nicholas, what on earth . . . ?"

There was no Nicholas.

Then she saw it. The light attached to the door. The cable attached to the light. The tape recorder attached to the cable. Yes, indeed, another one of Nicholas's marvelous inventions.

At first Mom didn't understand. Then it began to make

sense. It was all a trick. A sneaky trick to make them think he was in his room.

But why? Why would Nicholas want to deceive them like this?

She looked around the room and spotted the answer. On the bed. It was the newspaper advertisement for *Night of the Blood Freaks—Part IV*.

Mom was not smiling.

Back at the theater, the Blood Freaks had found that family and began attacking them . . . one at a time. The sounds were awful . . . lots of screaming and choking and gagging. But the sounds were nothing compared to what you watched. What Nicholas watched. What he couldn't take his eyes from.

As he watched, that volleyball came back into his stomach. Only now it wasn't content just to stay in his stomach. It was trying to jump up his throat and out his mouth. Nicholas tried his best to swallow it . . . but the worse the movie got, the harder it was to keep it down.

Finally everybody was killed off. Well, almost everybody. There was still one little member left. The tiny little sister. She cried; she whimpered; she begged . . . but nothing stopped the Blood Freaks. They did to her what they had done to the others. Only worse. Much worse. Much, much worse. Worse than much, much worse.

Then, just when Nick thought they had finished—just when he reached for his soda and tried to take a sip from his straw to settle his stomach—the Freaks finished their attack with this sickening slurp that sounded just like a soda straw getting the last little bit of drink in a cup.

Nick looked at his straw. Suddenly he wasn't so thirsty anymore.

EIGHT

BUSTED

At last the nightmare was over. The credits ended, and the final words on the screen were,

"Coming soon to a blood bank near you . . . *Blood Feast of the Blood Freaks—Part V.*"

The kids in the audience broke into cheers. Nick couldn't believe it. He glanced around. Everybody looked as sick and pale as he felt. They were wiped out too—but they were still cheering and clapping. It was like they could hardly wait to get grossed out all over again.

"Great flick, huh?" Louis beamed.

Nick tried to smile, but he wasn't too successful. Louis saw it, and for a second his grin also faded. For a second Nick could see what his friend was really thinking. Louis wasn't feeling so fit either. It lasted only a second, though.

"Hey, Louis," one of the kids from behind poked him in the back. "Wasn't that great the way they got that last kid?"

"Yeah." Louis was grinning again. "Or the way they . . ."

Nick didn't hear the rest of the conversation. Louis joined his friends and headed up the aisle. Everyone was laughing and talking and shouting. Nick just shook his head. No one would admit how frightened or scared they were. It was almost like they were trying too hard to prove they had had a good time.

But Nicholas couldn't fake it. He felt terrible. What had he done? And more important, why had he done it? His folks were right. The movie was awful. It was worse than awful. It was garbage. First-rate, triple-A garbage—with a lot of blood thrown in to wash it down.

The walk home took forever. Unfortunately forever wasn't quite long enough. . . .

When Nick rounded the corner of his block, he quickly checked his front yard. No one was there. So far, so good.

He reached the front porch and quietly crept up the steps. At the front door, he gave a careful listen. Nothing. The coast was clear. Maybe he could make it back up to his room without being noticed.

He opened the door. It gave a little squeak, but not much. He silently moved down the hall toward the stairs.

Then he spotted them.

They were on the kitchen table, and it wasn't good. There, piled in humiliation, were his cables, his tape recorder, and all of his other electronic gizmos.

The jig was up.

"Nicholas?" It was Dad. He was sitting in the family room. Apparently he had heard the squeaky door. At that moment, Nick hated that door. His dad's voice was cool and collected. Too cool and collected. "Come in here," he ordered.

Nicholas swallowed hard and obeyed. Slowly, though . . . very slowly.

"Sit down."

There was no mistaking that tone of voice. That was the tone that said, "I'm not going to yell; I'm not going to holler. I'm going to deal with this in a quiet, civilized manner." In other words, Nick was going to get it, and he was going to get it good.

If that wasn't bad enough, there was Mom. She was sitting across the coffee table pretending to read her *Ladies' Home Journal.* However, by the way she was flipping through the pages, you knew she wasn't really seeing them. In fact, she wasn't really seeing anything—except red.

"Were you at the movies?" Dad asked.

For the briefest second, Nick thought about lying. He could say he heard about a gigantic traffic accident on the radio . . . that he'd run downtown to give all the victims mouth-to-mouth resuscitation and save hundreds of lives. Or he could say that, out his window, he'd seen a jet airliner lose its wing in the air . . . he'd raced to the airport to talk the pilot down to a safe landing. Or maybe they'd believe he had suddenly found a cure for cancer and had to rush down to the hospital so not one more life would be lost.

All these thoughts flashed through his mind in a few seconds. But Nick decided the truth would be better. He'd done enough deceiving for one day.

Besides, if he told the truth, maybe they'd let him off easy. You know, something light like life imprisonment.

"Yes, sir," he answered his dad's question, barely above a whisper.

"Did you enjoy yourself?" his dad asked.

Again it was time for the truth. "No, sir . . . it was awful."

Mom and Dad exchanged looks.

Finally Mom spoke up. "Do you realize what you've done?" she asked.

Nicholas couldn't look up. He couldn't look into their eyes. He could only look at the ground.

"Son . . ." It was Dad now. "When your mother and I said you couldn't see that movie, we had a purpose."

Nick wanted to say something. He wanted to say that he understood now, that he knew their purpose. But no words came to mind. There was nothing but a tightness forming in the back of his throat. A tightness he couldn't swallow away.

"We wanted to protect you," Mom said.

"Nicholas. Look at me," Dad said quietly. "Nicholas."

It was hard, but at last the boy raised his head. He knew that what his dad was about to say was very important. He knew he'd better hear every word.

"Son," Dad continued, "your mind is the most important thing you have. That's why the Lord is so clear when he tells us to be careful what we put into it."

The boy continued to hold his dad's gaze. He would not, could not, look away.

Dad continued, "Whether you enjoyed that movie or not is beside the point. By going to see it, you've allowed something to come into your mind . . . to corrupt it . . . to dirty it."

Nick knew exactly what Dad meant. Boy, did he know.

Then it was Mom's turn. "There are scenes inside you now that you'll never be able to erase," she said. Nick could tell how much this upset her by the sad tone of her voice. "Pictures that may stay with you the rest of your life."

Suddenly Nick's eyes started to burn. He wanted to say something. He wanted to let them know what he was feeling. But there were only two words that came to mind. Two words that captured what he felt about disobeying them, about deceiving them, and about seeing the movie. . . .

"I'm sorry," he whispered hoarsely.

There was a moment of silence. They knew he meant it. Finally Dad answered. "I'm sorry, too, Son." Another moment, then Dad continued. "Now I want you to go up to your room and give this some thought. I'll be up in a little while to talk about your punishment."

Nicholas nodded slightly and rose to his feet. The movie had been awful, there was no doubt about that. What had been even more awful, though, was knowing how he'd disappointed his parents, how he'd let them down. As he turned, hot tears spilled onto his cheeks.

His back was to Mom and Dad, so they couldn't see his face . . . but it wouldn't have mattered. They were too busy fighting back the moisture in their own eyes to have seen his.

Being a kid is tough, no doubt about it. Being a parent who loves your child enough to do what's best—even when it hurts both of you—well, that's probably even tougher.

NINE

WRAPPING UP

Been many a day since he's seen the sun,
got no time to play,
got no time for fun.
'Cause he's having to pay for the things he's done.
Quiet as a mouse.
When Mom and Dad said no,
snuck out to see a scary movie.
That's how he found out
Ya reap what ya sow.

The following week found us reaping the "rewards" of our caper. As punishment for sneaking out of the house, Nick had to do various chores around the house.

He was in the middle of hauling a big load of boxes up to the attic when he stopped in the kitchen for a well-deserved drink. I, of course, was helping out by taking the demanding job of "Chief Supervisor in Charge of Personnel." I had positioned myself atop the kitchen table. Someone had to make sure the box-hauling journey from the garage to the attic went smoothly for my young friend.

As Nick downed a second glass of water, I tightened the straps on my work gloves and hitched up my support belt another notch. *(You can never be too careful when it comes to hard physical labor.)*

"Whew! I need a break," Nick said, wiping his brow and setting the glass down on the table.

"So, are we finished?" I asked.

"No, we are not finished. I still have to haul the rest of these boxes from the garage to the attic."

Despite his tone of voice, I knew Nick was really glad to have my help. He just doesn't show his feelings that much.

"Boy, the folks are riding you kind of hard, aren't they?" I commented.

"It could be worse," Nick said. "I could have to sit through that stupid movie again."

We both laughed. Sitting through that movie had been the most agonizing two hours of our lives (except maybe for the time we had to go to the aluminum-siding and storm-door expo with Mr. Dad). Anyway, hauling boxes was a picnic by comparison.

"I tell you, McGee, I'm through watching garbage like that," Nick said. I smiled. The experiences of the last few days had really taught him a valuable lesson. "But you gotta help me," he added. "That kind of stuff is all around."

Of course, I would be glad to help my little pal. After all, it's easier to stick to your guns when you've got somebody standing beside you.

"Yeah, it's tough making the right choices," I answered. "But it's like I always told you: The road to ruin is paved with crude inventions."

Nick rolled his eyes and grinned slightly as he got up

and gathered the boxes he had dumped on the kitchen table. "Inventions!" he said, laughing. "You mean like the time you told me to use Mom's vacuum cleaner to rake the yard?"

"It would have worked if you hadn't hit the sprinkler," I said, scooping some raspberry jam out of the jar next to me.

Nick just shook his head and started hauling the boxes toward the stairs. "Or how about the time you told me to cut the sleeves off my shirt so Mom wouldn't see where I tore it? Or the time . . ." His voice trailed off in the distance as he headed up the stairs.

Sure, I remembered all those things. It was clear Nick had a great memory too. It was clear that it could take some time to put the last few days behind us. And believe me, that movie and Nick's "escape" were things I would just as soon forget.

One thing was sure, though: Nick and I would have a lot more memories—some good, some bad. If we were smart, we'd use all of them to make the road ahead a little easier to follow. Or at least a little clearer. Knowing Nick and me, that road would be paved with fun, friendship, and above all, adventure.

Stay tuned, sports fans. . . .